Jericho's Journey

by G. Clifton Wisler

Puffin Books

PUFFIN BOOKS
Published by the Penguin Group
Penguin Books USA Inc., 375 Hudson Street, New York, New York 10014, U.S.A.
Penguin Books Ltd, 27 Wrights Lane, London W8 5TZ, England
Penguin Books Australia Ltd, Ringwood, Victoria, Australia
Penguin Books Canada Ltd, 10 Alcorn Avenue, Toronto, Ontario, Canada M4V 3B2
Penguin Books (N.Z.) Ltd, 182–190 Wairau Road, Auckland 10, New Zealand

Penguin Books Ltd, Registered Offices: Harmondsworth, Middlesex, England

First published in the United States of America by Lodestar Books,
an affiliate of Dutton Children's Books,
a division of Penguin Books USA Inc., 1993
Published in Puffin Books, 1995

9 10

THE LIBRARY OF CONGRESS HAS CATALOGED THE LODESTAR BOOKS EDITION AS FOLLOWS:
Wisler, G. Clifton.
Jericho's journey / G. Clifton Wisler.—1st ed.
p.   cm.
Summary: As his family makes the long and difficult journey from
Tennessee to their new home in Texas in 1852,
twelve-year-old Jericho Wetherby, teased by his sister and
brothers about his size, learns there are many ways to grow.
ISBN 0-525-67428-4
[1. Frontier and pioneer life—Fiction. 2. Brothers and
sisters—Fiction. 3. Size—Fiction.] I. Title.
PZ7.W78033Je   1993   [Fic]—dc20   92-36701   CIP   AC

Puffin Books ISBN 0-14-037065-X
Printed in the United States of America

for my Scouting friends

CHAPTER ONE

I WAS BORN AND GROWN FOUR AND A HALF FEET TALL before I got more than fifty miles from Roane County, Tennessee. Even then it was only bouncing along in the back of Grandpa Fitch's wagon, squeezed in with a dozen baskets of peaches bound for market in Knoxville. I didn't note much of interest getting there, and I slept most of the way back home. So as far as adventures go, it wasn't anything to boast on.

That was peculiar, too. On the whole, Wetherbys have always been wanderers. Since coming across the Atlantic way back in the time of King James, our people have been creeping westward by degrees. Greatgrandpa Wetherby came through Cumberland Gap after the Revolution, and my own pa rode down from the mountains to Roane County when he was just sixteen or so. As for Ma's people, the Fitches, she had brothers in Missouri, New Orleans—and Texas!

Texas! Now there was a word to stir the blood. My Uncle Dan set off for that country back in 1836 when the place was still a part of Mexico.

"Just seventeen," Ma liked to tell me. "Fence-rail skinny, and a far cry from mustering a beard. Hair as rooster red as yours, Jericho, and a hair-trigger temper to match. That's how I recall Dan the day he shouldered his rifle and set off to fight for freedom."

To be truthful, Uncle Dan got to Texas after the fighting was all over, but he did serve a month or so in some sort of militia. The country was thankful enough to give him a nice stretch of land, and he was forever writing us about the rich black prairie and fine creeks where he lived.

"Bold-faced lies!" Grandpa Fitch declared. "There's nothing but ruin and heartache to be found in Texas! The place is full of land thieves and savages. One'll pick your pocket and the other's sure to take your hair."

Grandpa didn't think much of the place, judging it too hot for growing good peach trees. On the other hand, Pa had been dreaming about Texas for as long as I could remember. Summer evenings we'd all of us gather out back beneath the tulip trees and listen to yarns. Most were about Daniel Boone or Davy Crockett, real Tennessee heroes. Sooner or later he'd squeeze in a word about Texas, though.

"Ole Davy died at the Alamo, you know," Pa would say, and I'd settle in with my brothers and sister, knowing we were in for a long night of it.

So you see how, even at eleven, I knew plenty about Texas. I could about draw you a map of the Alamo, that old Spanish mission where Davy and the other heroes had died fighting the Mexican army back in 1836. And I'd even met General Sam Houston, who passed by once in a coach bound for Washington, D.C., where he was due to be a senator. Was Houston, you know, who'd surprised the Mexican general Santa Anna and captured his whole army.

Pa was fond of telling how the Texans knew it was ole Santa Anna on account of his wearing silk underwear. I won't vouch for the truth of the tale, but Ma sure did get red-faced to hear such talk, and my little brothers Jordy and Josh cackled like magpies afterward.

But in spite of the letters Uncle Dan sent Ma and the tales Pa shared most every chance he had, Texas was a distant dream. I figured to have an equal chance of spying Texas and climbing the mountains of the moon.

"Dreaming's for Sundays," my sister Jane Mary grumbled as she rooted us out of our beds each morning. "Climb into those overalls and get after your chores, boys!"

To hear her give orders, you'd judge she was old Sam Houston herself. She wasn't but fourteen, and more than a hair puny. When she chose, Jane Mary could slip on a calico dress and comb out her nutmeg-colored hair so you'd deem her almost pretty. But mostly she stuck her nose in books, which was fine by me, for it kept her sharp tongue indoors and far away from me.

"You boys would do well to adopt your sister's manners," Ma sometimes scolded.

"Aren't enough little ones for two Jane Marys to boss," my big brother Jake observed. "Lucky she didn't come by Jer's red hair, though. Ill-tempered and ornery both! Now that'd be the devil's match for sure."

Jake was one to talk! He was only fifteen, and a bit stunted, as Ma's people, the Fitches, were prone to getting their growth late. Jake could find more ways to stir up trouble than a barn full of hornets. Lately he'd grown worse, partly because Meg Neely, the pretty daughter of the miller up the road, spurred him to mischief. She and the Claggett gals, whose pa had the next farm upriver, were terrible taken with Jake, and one of them was sending supper invites around regular.

"Don't you think he's grown handsome?" Sara Claggett asked me once.

"To my eye, he hasn't grown much at all," I answered. Jake gave me a good whack for that, but afterward he made amends.

"Can't expect a man to be altogether sensible where women's involved," Jake told me. Still, it was hard to see how a brother could turn so mean over a skinny Claggett gal. We'd been spying on them bathing in the

4

river since any of us could remember, and I hadn't noticed much to attract the eye. Jake was pure crazed by the gals, though, and afterward I kept mum when one was around. I'd never confess it to him, but I admired Jake considerably. He was the best rifle shot I ever saw, and he could outrun anybody. I once saw him knock a dove out of a tree with a slingshot, and he was truly a wonder on horseback. I couldn't abide him being riled with me.

That particular summer my little brothers and I didn't see too much of Jake. He was of an age and size to help Pa with the harder work, and when he wasn't working the cornfield, he was certain to be romancing Meg or one of the Claggetts. That left me, Jordy, and Josh to tend our army of hogs and chickens.

Now as little brothers go, my two weren't the worst. No, hearing Jake's tales of Sterling Claggett, who was eight like Josh, made me downright grateful. Jordy, now he was ten, was becoming a fair companion on adventures. If he was painfully quiet sometimes, he never shirked his share of the work, and he was wonderful around animals. Why, he could walk among the hogs and not get smashed, and he even got along with the chickens!

"Jordy could coax an egg out of a rooster," Jake told me once. I don't suppose that was altogether possible, but Jordy never got his feet pecked, which is more than I could say for myself.

As to Josh, we all worried after him some. He was

smallish even by Fitch standards, and ghostly pale. He took sick every winter, and sometimes even in summer.

"He was a late-birthed baby," Grandma Fitch told me once. "Those are always prone to ail more than others."

Ma lost a pair of twin boys at birth last summer, and my little brother Jeremiah, who folks liked to compare to me, drowned in the river the summer before that. So when Josh took to his bed, we all bent our knees and prayed hard. By and by he coughed himself well.

Most days I didn't think on such sour events. Summer was a fine time for adventures, and whenever we got our chores finished early, we'd escape Jane Mary's attention and head down to the river for a swim or some other foolishness. More than once we provided a basket of fat Tennessee River catfish for supper. And sometimes we'd snare a rabbit. It wasn't like hunting with Jake and coming in with muskrats or coons, but Ma could make rabbit taste good as a pork roast, and we younger boys deemed ourselves true Wetherbys when we filled the supper pot.

So I'd say it wasn't altogether unusual to find Jordy, Josh, and me down at the river on an August afternoon. I'd like to claim we'd gone down there to scare up a catfish or hunt rabbits, but the truth was it had turned Tennessee hot, and we took to the water to wring the sweat and weariness out of us. We were racing one another from one bank to the other, yelling and raising cain, when Jake happened along.

"Guess the hogs all been fed, huh?" he called. "And the kindling box's full?"

"Mostly," I answered, avoiding his eyes. "And there's time to finish when we're through here. Ma thought it a good idea if the little ones had a wash."

"Funny that," Jake said, scratching his chin. "I guess she forgot to send the soap along."

"All used up," Jordy claimed.

"I'll believe that," Jake said, "the day Miranda Hopkins rides buff naked into Knoxville."

We had ourselves a good laugh at that thought. Miz Hopkins was the spinster sister of the sheriff, and she was sixty years of wrinkles on a good day.

"You come down here to get onto us for neglecting chores?" I asked.

"No," he confessed, grinning. "That would be Jane Mary's work."

We all breathed a trifle easier. Looking Jake over, I could tell, too, he hadn't expected to find us at all. He'd greased his yellow hair shiny and put on a clean blue cotton shirt under his overall straps.

"Coming in?" Josh called to him.

"After bigger fish," Jake answered, glancing upriver.

I imagined him walking with Sara or Abigail Claggett, and I near choked.

"Don't you go taking up Jake's example," Grandpa Fitch had scolded me once. "That boy's a born rascal and will surely prove a worry to his family."

I'd nodded soberly, thinking all the while about the wild adventures Jake would have along the way.

Jake didn't seem himself just then, though.

"You lovesick or something?" Jordy asked.

"Headed over to the Claggetts," I said, laughing.

"Thought to," Jake confessed. "Got some serious words to share with them."

"About what?" Josh asked, splashing over and sitting in the shallows.

"Pa's talking about going to Texas," Jake explained.

"So when isn't he?" I asked. "Ever since Uncle Dan went there, before any of us was even born, Pa's been figuring to leave. Hasn't yet."

"Doesn't mean he won't," Jake told us. "Pa had a fellow out to look the farm over this morning. They talked money and such. Seems a new letter came from Uncle Dan."

Uncle Dan's letters told of some high times—wild horse hunts and fearsome Indian raids. To be truthful, I was sometimes scared halfway out of my pants by those tales. Grandpa Fitch had warned us plenty about that wild country full of Indians and bandits. Even so, it promised adventure aplenty, and a boy of eleven will take that anytime.

"Would it be so awful, going to Texas?" Jordy asked. "This place has gotten awful tame, and Texas is full of adventures."

"And danger," Jake warned, looking older. "Ma's not so well, you know."

We did know. She hadn't been altogether healthy since losing the little twins. Born one day and dead the next.

"Might be she'd do better in a new place," I declared. "Less around to remind her."

"Maybe," Jake admitted. "But I heard folks talk about the trip. Plenty of rivers to cross, and pitiful few good roads. We couldn't leave before getting in the harvest, so it would be winter 'fore we got there. That's a season of chills and fevers. No time to be without a good house."

"Won't happen," Jordy said, glancing at Josh.

Jake only shrugged his shoulders. He didn't look any too convinced. As for me, I was confused. Wasn't it Jake who was forever setting off on coon and squirrel hunts? He enjoyed Pa's Texas yarns more than the rest of us put together. So why the fretting?

Jake headed on along then, and we younger Wetherbys climbed the bank, shook ourselves dry, and got dressed. We passed the rest of the afternoon doing chores—mainly carrying water to the house and chopping stove wood.

At supper we gathered like always. But Grandpa and Grandma Fitch had come out to join us, and Ma set the table with her good china plates. Platters of roast pork, sweet potatoes, peas, and carrots crowded the sideboard. There was a peach pie cooling beside the oven, too.

"It's not Sunday, is it?" Josh whispered to me. I shook my head, and he squeezed in beside me on the hard oak bench that we boys shared.

Grandma waited for us to join hands. Then she said grace. We all waited a respectful minute afterward before starting in on the food. There wasn't anything like chopping wood to stir up a hunger, and I stuffed myself proper.

We were well into the pie when Grandpa started in on Texas.

"Now that's just not true," Pa argued. "Dan's done wonderfully well there." Pa set down his fork and glanced around the big oak table where Ma and we children were shaking our heads and hoping the talk would pass.

"Dan never had the sense to know when he was well off," Grandpa muttered. "He could have had his granny's farm if he had the backbone to work. Instead he headed off on his fool adventure and near got his foot shot off fighting Comanches!"

"Pa, Dan's got a fine ranch now," Ma pointed out. "And he's bought land north and west that he's offered us at a fine price."

"Four hundred dollars," Pa said, smiling. "For six hundred acres and change, with a cabin already up, a good stream nearby, and more than enough timber to provide firewood."

"There's a wonderful future waiting for us in Collin County," Ma declared, waving Uncle Dan's latest letter in the air. "It's a fresh beginning. Something for the young ones."

"They've got a future right here," Grandpa insisted. "Somebody will take on my orchards. I won't live forever, you know."

"And the others?" Pa asked. "Even in a good year this place scarcely pays our debts. That's sure to get worse. Jake'll be shaving before long, and Jericho's closing in on twelve," Pa said, throwing a glance my way. "They'll be wanting more of a life than planting corn and slopping hogs."

"There's work around," Grandpa said. "I don't see any whiskers sprouting on Jake."

"They're there," Jake complained, scratching his chin. Pa grinned, and Jane Mary laughed. "Just hard to see," Jake mumbled.

"I see 'em," I whispered. Jake elbowed me quiet.

"You don't know what a journey like that means," Grandma said, dabbing her eyes with a cloth. "I was just a girl myself when my people came through Cumberland Gap from Virginia. First winter we lost my baby sister, and a bear killed my brother George. Wasn't as old as Jericho there. Coming to Tennessee cost me enough. Texas will take the rest."

She waved her hand at us, and Ma paled.

"Joe Wetherby, don't you bring down calamity on these children," Grandma pleaded. "Nor on Mary Elizabeth. Hasn't she known sorrow enough?"

"Too much sorrow," Pa declared. "Texas promises a fresh start."

I looked at Pa, then at Ma. I knew what they were thinking. Every walk past the river brought memories of Jeremiah. He was buried fifty feet from the house, he and the dead twins. Wasn't any forgetting possible with them so close!

"I'll be shorthanded come picking time," Grandpa

claimed. "No young fingers to help. Just be the two of us."

Jake's toes nervously tapped the floor, and I now realized what was worrying him. He feared being left behind.

"No, Pa," Ma said, smiling. "It's all thought out. Mr. Haskell, who's offered to buy the farm, has youngsters eager to do the work."

"And what of your corn?" Grandpa asked.

"We'll stay through harvest," Pa promised. "That should give us time to put everything in order."

"Dan said he needs four hundred for the farm," Grandpa said, folding his napkin. "You'll require a good wagon. Horses, too. Art Perkins has four good Morgans. He'll hold them dear, but he owes half Roane County money. They'll be my gift to get you started proper."

"You'll have Mother's chest, too," Grandma added. "The blue English china. When Jane Mary weds, it can pass on to her."

"Bless you, Ma," Ma managed.

"Won't be much for the boys," Grandpa said, scratching his ear. "But then starting new like you are, bunch of old things would just weigh you down."

"More for the thieves to steal, too," Grandma muttered.

"You should take a pair of good roosters and such hens as you can," Grandpa continued. "Hogs don't travel well, but you'll want a good milk cow . . . ole

Cathy will do. Jericho's certain to want my fool collie dog along."

"Sandy!" I yelped. "Thank you, Grandpa."

"It's little enough," he said, nodding with sad eyes. "And don't you boys go Texas wild on me just yet. You won't leave till the corn crop's in, and that's a way off. Mostly you're taking Fitch backbone along. I hope to have given you plenty of that, all right."

"Yes, sir," we all agreed.

"This county will be too quiet," Grandma said, dabbing her eyes again. "You children don't write regular, I'll die early and come haunting you. I will, too."

"Yes, ma'am," Josh said with wide eyes. "Soon's we find paper."

"I mean you, too, Jericho," Grandma added. "I've given up saving Jake there from the gallows, but you might have the makings of a churchgoer yet."

"I wouldn't wager on it, Grandma," Jordy said, laughing at my fidgeting.

"Any more talk of wagering, it will be you I take after," she replied. "You're not so big I can't take a switch to you, Jordan Wetherby."

We all had a good laugh at that notion.

"Now, we've had about enough talk for one night," Grandma announced. "Finish up your pie there, Jordy. Josh, wipe your chin, dear. Jane Mary, help me clear away the dishes."

"Yes, ma'am," Jane Mary said, standing and taking

the roast pork platter. "Hurry up now, Jericho. Your turn with the dishes."

I only half groaned at the news, for Pa was lit up with a smile bright as July sunlight.

"I'll help," Jordy volunteered, and I hurried to finish my pie. Shortly we were scraping plates clean and making up Texas adventures.

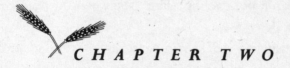

CHAPTER TWO

TEXAS WAS STILL A LONG WAYS OFF. SEEMED TO ME EVERY time I turned around the trip got delayed another week. First, Grandpa was a fair time haggling over the price of those Morgan horses. Then too, we had a bumper corn crop. By the time we gathered in the ears and got them sold, October was staring us in the face.

Most times I welcomed October. The weather cooled, for one thing. Also I had my twelfth birthday the first day of that month, and for once I got some attention. Sure, it was mostly pranks played on me by one brother or another, but at least I wasn't ignored.

"Twelve, huh?" Pa said when he looked me over at breakfast. "Appears to me these boys all take after the Fitches, Ma. Puny to a fault."

"We're not all that small," Jordy objected.

"Not unless you take to considering brains," Jane Mary said, laughing.

"Size, huh?" Jake said. "I know one girl who's got her share of size, mouthwise anyhow."

Jane Mary about walloped him. Jake had a year and three months on her, but she had three good inches and ten pounds in her favor. All of it was meanness, too. No fat on that girl! I could testify to the fact because that meanness generally settled itself on top of me. Jake could outrun a bobcat, but Jane Mary would pounce on me regular.

"Poor little Jericho," she'd tease as I wriggled underneath her bony knees. "Aren't you going to cry this time?"

"I'm through with crying!" I'd holler. And no matter how hard she twisted my arms or how many times she stomped my ribs, I wouldn't shed a tear.

It being my birthday, she mainly turned her sharp tongue on Jake. On toward suppertime, though, that changed. We were a big family, and neither the Wetherbys nor the Fitches was prone to making much of occasions. Pa fixed me up with a worn pair of shoes passed down from Jake. Ma gave me a new calico shirt she'd sewn big to last out the winter. And Grandpa Fitch handed over a keen pair of razors I figure he'd saved for some later birthday.

"One's for Jake," he whispered. "I expect he'll need it after Christmas."

I grinned at the thought, for Jake was clearly fuming.

"What's Jericho to do with those?" Jane Mary asked, turning on me with a sneer. "Why, he's not even got hairs to shave off his legs!"

"I expect he'll save 'em up for whiskers," Grandpa said, scowling at Jane Mary. "That or shave his skull like some wild Indian. Plenty of those up Texas way, I understand. Now you hush yourself, granddaughter!"

It was like spitting on a fire, though. Jane Mary saw the words stung, and she kept after me all evening.

"Little Jer," she whined over and over. "Twelve? Why, I've seen snails bigger."

"Don't you let such talk bother you," Ma told me when she found me staring at the moon that night.

"Wouldn't hurt if there wasn't truth to it," I replied. "Bet I didn't grow an inch this whole entire year!"

"That's how it was with your Uncle Dan," she explained. "Sort of saved up his growing. Then, come fourteen, he shot up like a pine tree, almost overnight. You favor him, you know."

"Jake's fifteen, and he's not done any big growing," I complained. "No, we're just puny, like Pa says."

"Pure bilge water, that is," she said, resting a hand on my shoulder. "Your pa's proud of the way you shoulder your share of the work. He'll have even more cause to be proud before we reach Texas. Long trip like that grows you taller."

"Not me," I grumbled.

"Lots of ways to grow tall," she whispered. "Watch and see if I'm not right."

"We ever leaving?" I asked.

"Before the week's out," she announced. "Your pa's got the harness ready for the Morgans, and the corn crop's sold. Wagon's sure to be here tomorrow. And now your grandpa's given over his razors, I can't think much else's left to get done."

"Just good-byes," I mumbled.

"Yes, there's that," she agreed.

Me, though, I didn't bid many farewell. I'd hoped to get along up the river and talk to the Perkins boys. Then I'd have words with the Claggetts. But there was so much to do the time flew right past. I helped Pa build a chicken coop onto the back of the wagon, and Jake and I built a tool box for the axes and hoes and such onto the right side. We hung a good plow made of Tennessee hickory in a cradle on the opposite side, sandwiched between our water barrels.

Pa had us finish the loading an hour shy of dawn on a crisp Thursday morning, the seventh day of October. After a big breakfast, he wrote considerable in the family Bible, ending it with "Gone to Texas, 1852."

"I guess that means you're really leaving," Grandma Fitch sobbed as she hugged us each in turn.

I nodded. After all, the back of the wagon was loaded with Great-grandma's chest, Ma and Pa's cannonball bed, a spinning wheel, flour and sugar sacks, powder and shot, and such clothes as we owned, each thing in its assigned place. Back of the seat two long percussion-cap rifles and four cane fishing poles stood ready.

I made my way around the circle of family and friends that showed up at daybreak to wish us well. I had a hug for Grandma Fitch and some of the neighbor ladies, and I shook hands with Mr. Haskell, who was taking over the farm. Grandpa squeezed my shoulders, wished me well, and bid me take good care of Sandy, the collie dog that was pacing beside the wagon, ready to get going.

"Where's Mary Elizabeth got to?" Grandma asked as she waved a feather cushion. "I've ridden these fool spring wagons. Mostly it's your back does the springing! See your ma uses this, hear!" she told Jordy.

I knew where Ma was, and I slipped away from the others and hurried there myself. Sure enough, she was sitting on the cold ground beside the three carved boards that marked the graves of my brothers.

"I think Pa's ready," I whispered as I stood beside her.

"This is the hardest farewell of all," she told me. I noticed the tears in her eyes and dropped my chin onto my chest. Wasn't anything I could have done about the twins, but if I'd been a better swimmer, I might've fished Jeremiah out of the river and squeezed the water out of him.

"More'n once I wished it was me instead of him," I said, sighing. "Might be he'd got proper tall."

"Was God called my boys to Him," she insisted. "It's not for us to question."

"Hurts just the same."

"Life hurts," she told me. "But by and by it brings you joy, too. Say your good-byes and hurry along. Won't do to keep your pa waiting."

"No, ma'am," I agreed.

I knelt beside the graves and whispered a word or two. Mainly I told Jeremiah I was sorry he'd never see Texas. And as I walked away, I hoped Preacher Mackay was right about heaven being a fine place, with harp playing and golden streets. Wasn't a warming thought, thinking on resting forever in that cold rocky Tennessee ground.

I turned and raced back to the wagon just in time. Pa was mounting his buckskin gelding, Dandy, and Ma was perched atop the wagon seat. The horses snorted and stomped. They were clearly ready to get to work.

"God speed you to your destination!" Grandma hollered, and we waved a final farewell. Then Ma whipped the horses into motion, and I raced after Sandy. Jake rode along on Red, Pa's fine roan mare, and I was pure green with envy. Still, chasing Sandy was better than walking along with Jane Mary tormenting you. For once she'd turned her meanness on Josh and Jordy.

"Good-bye, house!" Jordy yelled.

"Good-bye, river!" Josh added.

"Howdy, Texas!" Jake called as he galloped by.

But like I said, Texas was a long way off. And we had considerable traveling ahead of us.

* * *

We didn't get far that first day. Two miles, Pa said. It was growing cold, and the skies were clouding over, so we stopped at the Edding place and camped beside the river crossing.

I don't think anybody except Pa minded halting early. Ma, cushion or not, had taken her share of bouncing. Josh and Jordy were complaining of their feet and Jane Mary, not exactly in that order. My own feet were sore, but it was my back ached——from lifting and toting.

Life didn't get easier right away, either. Pa headed over to talk Mr. Edding out of such supplies as he warranted we didn't yet have, and he was a full hour dickering. Jake and I unhitched the horses and set up a canvas shelter where we boys would pass the night. Wasn't room in the wagon for much of anybody, but Ma, Pa, and Jane Mary would sleep there.

When Pa returned, he gave me oats to feed the horses, and Ma started slicing up a ham. Jake dragged over a fallen hickory and began chopping it into firewood. As for Jordy and Josh, they busied themselves naming the horses.

"Can't ask a horse to pull a wagon and not give it a name," Jordy insisted.

"Well, it will give Pa something to call 'em," Jake agreed. "Or to cuss anyway."

"Not with Ma there beside him," Jordy pointed out. "And anyhow, those horses pulled good."

"Better'n you two walked," Jane Mary said, trotting

over to grab wood for the fire. "That all, Jer? I don't guess those puny arms are good for anything!"

"Might be strong enough to strangle a sister," I muttered once she was gone.

We ate ourselves an early supper that night. Pa was determined we get an early start next day, and he worried we might have a lot of unwanted company.

"Edding says the crossing draws all sorts of folks," Pa warned. "Jake, you especially keep close to camp. I don't want you mixing with a bunch of gamblers and ne'er-do-wells."

I saw Jake's eyes catch fire. You might as well have set coal oil onto a candle! And it wasn't much after sundown that Jake set off to explore the music coming from a tent camp upriver.

Me, I feared he'd land himself in trouble, going off alone like that, so I trailed along. He frowned some when he spotted me, but he didn't send me back. Instead the two of us climbed a hill and looked down on the gamblers' camp. It was a lively place, all right, with half-dressed women dancing around, and three whole tables of card players going at it. A whiskey seller ended up with the lion's share of the cash, for he was peddling bottles right and left.

"What say, Jer?" Jake asked after a time. "Got any money? I might just have myself a go at them fellows."

"Got some pennies is all," I answered. "They're back in the wagon, too."

"All I got's four bits," he said, frowning. "Can't buy much with that."

"Just as well," Pa said, resting one hand on each of our shoulders. I guess we both jumped five feet in the air, howling like boys set upon by some haunt. Good thing the gamblers liked loud music or we might have sent them running, fearing bandits—or worse.

"Sorry, Pa," I managed to plead. "We just had to have ourselves a look."

"Sure," he said, betraying a trace of smile. "You had one. Now to bed with you both. And no more wandering, hear?"

"No, sir," I said.

Jake nodded, but I saw he had his fingers crossed.

We returned with Pa, hanging our heads in pretended remorse. But later, when Pa doused the lantern and climbed into the wagon, Jordy and Josh begged a tale out of us. Jake turned our foray into a regular adventure. I especially admired him for the way he had those ladies welcoming him into their camp.

The story ended by and by, and we rolled out our blankets and climbed out of our overalls. The air was already cool, and the wind turned it cold. Jake was asleep fast, like always, and Jordy drifted off a hair later. Little Josh burrowed his way into my side, and for a few minutes he shivered. Then the wool blanket chased off the chill, and he settled down.

I had a hard time finding rest, though. At first the noise from the gamblers' camp bothered me. Later, when they quieted themselves, it was too silent. Then I began to hear the sounds of the woods, and I slid over nearer Jake. Josh rolled over so he near crushed my leg, and I had to slide him off me.

You would have thought I'd be all right. Wasn't a finger of space between the four of us now, and even a fool knew nothing could get to me without passing Josh or Jake first. All of a sudden every old haunt tale and spook yarn I'd ever heard came back on me. I imagined cutthroats and river pirates, one-eyed bandits and hairy giants—all coming after me!

It got worse. For just as I was about to shake myself out of my blankets, something cold touched my bare toe.

"Nooo," I moaned, sitting up and praying no demon had found our camp. It was just Sandy, though, come to share our warmth. I halfway laughed. Then there was a rustling in the brush just past our dead fire, and Sandy let loose a sharp bark. Instantly the collie turned and growled as a dark shape hunched over Ma's Dutch oven.

"Jake, wake up!" I howled as Sandy tore into the intruder. Wasn't a minute later the fool dog yelped in pain and dashed back to our shelter, nursing a bit paw.

"Jer?" Jake asked sleepily as I threw off my blankets and raced for the safety of the wagon. The moon dipped out of the clouds long enough for me to see two big green eyes peering over from the fire. There I was, bare-legged, half frozen, with only my shirt for protection. I remembered the rifles, though. I reached for one and pulled out a cane pole instead.

Our visitor let off a sort of clicking noise, then waddled closer. I was sure it was a bear escaped Davy Crockett's attention, and I recalled him saying the best thing to do was stare down critters. Problem was, in that darkness, I wasn't sure it could see me!

Nevertheless when it started after our flour sack, I swung my pole over and gave it a solid whack. That cane was no good, though. The critter swatted it and shattered the far end into slivers.

"What in tarnation?" Jake asked as he rubbed sleep out of his eyes.

"We got ourselves a bear!" I screamed.

Jake's eyes grew wide, and he jumped to his feet. Now Josh and Jordy were awake, too, and they started scrambling underneath the wagon.

"Bear!" Josh hollered.

"Bear!" Jordy echoed.

Jake was pretty calm, though. He climbed into the wagon, grabbed his rifle, and began loading it. By the time he'd rammed powder and ball down the barrel and fixed a percussion cap beneath the hammer, his eyes had adjusted to the dark. Meanwhile I was still fighting off the beast with what was left of the pole.

"Boys!" Pa shouted as he flung back the canvas wagon cover and stared down at us. "What—"

"Bear!" Josh yelled.

"Bear!" Jordy echoed again.

"Nonsense!" Pa grumbled. To be truthful, in that dim light he looked more bear than our visitor. He was six foot three, and I guess he weighed two hundred fifty pounds. He bellowed out, and that varmint at the fire retreated. Jake then aimed and fired. The shot near deafened me, and powder smoke stung my eyes.

"I got it!" Jake exclaimed as he raced forward.

"Hooray!" Jordy and Josh cried as they emerged from their hiding place.

"Fool boys!" Pa grumbled as he stepped down and motioned us to our blankets. "Jake, what did you shoot, boy? Sure wasn't any kind of bear."

"Just a coon," Jake said, holding the pitiful killed creature by its tail. "Big one, though. Thirty pounds easy."

"Likely stirred up half the county, shooting off that rifle," Pa complained as he pried the gun from Jake's hands. "Now it'll have to be cleaned and oiled. You dress that coon, too, Jake. I won't have meat wasted."

"Yes, sir," Jake answered.

"Waste of powder," Pa declared, shaking his head. "Powder comes dear, you know."

"It bit Sandy in the leg," I explained. "And was about to rip open the flour sack."

"That should have been put away," Pa told us. "See the food's stored properly from now on, boys. And don't go waking me in the middle of the night!"

"Yes, sir," Jake and I replied.

Pa muttered to himself as he returned to the wagon.

Jake collected what food remained out and stored it behind the seat atop the wagon. I dragged the dead coon over and lit the lantern up. Then Jake set to skinning the animal.

"Some bear," Jordy complained when he stepped over for a look.

"Well, it was a big coon," Josh said, gazing over at me sympathetically.

Sandy crept over, and Jake tossed some bones at the poor dog. I believe Sandy was more embarrassed than I was.

"I feel like a fool," I told Jake after the little ones went back to sleep.

"Don't," he urged. "Was you saved the flour. I'd have slept right along through it all. Anyhow, I fought my first battle, so to speak. And once I get this hide dried out, I'll have a skin cap. Be a regular Davy Crockett, don't you figure?"

"Sure, you will be," I agreed. "Maybe next time you shoot a coon, I can have the hide."

"Shoot your own coon," he grumbled. "Or better yet, find me a bear next time."

"Only if I can have a skin cap."

"All right," he said, moaning. "Get a game bag for this meat, will you? You know we'll end up eating coon stew tomorrow. Worst kind of tough, greasy meat in all creation."

"Grandma Fitch used to make a passable coon stew."

"Well, Ma makes it taste worse than shoe leather.

You wouldn't remember, but she cooked up a coon Pa shot once out past the river. Last time Grandpa let her at a coon, I'll tell you."

"Maybe we should feed it to Sandy," I suggested.

"Poor dog can't eat all thirty pounds, Jer. And we'd feel Pa's belt for wasting the meat."

"Sure," I admitted.

"Almost'd be worth it, though. Ma sure can't cook coon."

I found myself laughing at him. He peeled off the last of the skin, dressed the meat, and placed it in the bag I brought from the wagon. Jake then hung up the bag from a nearby hickory branch, and we went back to sleep. This time I drifted off in a flash and didn't wake before morning.

CHAPTER THREE

PA STIRRED ME TO LIFE AT DAYBREAK. I YAWNED AWAY MY weariness and shook off the morning chill. Beside me Jake roused Josh and Jordy and gave me a nudge in the side.

"Chores are waiting," he told me. "Get dressed."

I moaned some, but I did kick off my blanket, roll Josh off my leg, and pull on my overalls. Didn't take me a minute to get my new boots on, and afterward I hurried over to where Jake was building up a cook fire.

"Strange how it seems dawn comes earlier out here in the open," he said as he broke branches in two and made a tepee of sorts.

"Bound to get worse, too," I said, yawning again. "Before we get to Texas, we'll see frost."

"Maybe even snow," Jake said, frowning. "Wish it was spring. Fall's fever season."

I followed his eyes back to the shelter where Josh and Jordy were slowly getting dressed. If I was puny, they were downright skeletons! I do believe the wagon spokes had more meat than those boys' legs. Jake scowled, and I judged he was thinking the same thing.

"You boys got that fire started yet?" Pa called from the wagon.

"Just doing it now," Jake answered as he pulled a ball of lint from his tinder pouch and struck the handle of his knife to a slice of black flint. The third spark caught the lint on fire, and soon the drier branches ignited. Some were wet with dew, and they mostly smoked, but eventually a small fire started up. We piled on bigger branches and held our hands over the flames.

I felt warmth spread through my arms, and I inhaled the odor of wood smoke. Soon Ma would be frying up ham and eggs, maybe even biscuits. I felt my insides twist and turn as hunger set in.

"I'll tend the fire," Jane Mary volunteered as she stepped over. "Pa's got other chores for the two of you."

"Other chores?" Jake asked.

"We just got through building the fire," I complained.

"Well, Ma and I'll be cooking," she replied. "You do want to eat, don't you? Hurry and get to work."

"Isn't that what we've been doing?" I muttered. Jake

grabbed my arm, though, and hauled me to the wagon. Ma was slicing her ham, and Pa was looking after the horses.

"Get along to Edding's store," Pa instructed. "I bought some supplies. They're up there waiting. Bring 'em down and get 'em stashed proper."

"Yes, sir," Jake said, starting up the hill toward the Edding place. I reluctantly followed.

Mr. Edding's store stood right alongside his cabin. I half expected we'd have a wait for the supplies, seeing as how it was scarcely daybreak. But by the time Jake and I got there, Edding's boys were busy loading a pair of wagons.

"You the Wetherby boys?" Mr. Edding called.

"Yes, sir," Jake answered.

"There's your boxes on the porch," the storekeeper explained.

I followed Jake. He took one look at the boxes and frowned.

"There's a hundred pounds of flour here," he said, shaking his head. "And what's this?"

"A skillet lid," I said, picking it up. The fool thing was cast iron and weighed as much as my whole arm.

"You can use it like a griddle," a familiar voice explained. I glanced up and spied a spindle-legged, dark-haired boy about my age sitting on a barrel. It was Henry Avery, who lived on one of the farms upriver.

"What's brought you out this way, Henry?" I asked.

"Hauling grain," Henry said with a shrug. "Pa and

me. Headed for Chattanooga. Hear the price's better down that way."

"That's a fair trip," Jake said, nodding. "But not as far as Texas."

"Texas?" Henry asked.

"Texas," I answered. "We're headed there. Whole family."

"Texas, huh? Now that's a place I'd like to see," Henry told us. "Wild country, they say. Got a cousin going there. Eli Grady."

"I know Eli," Jake said, nodding. "He's what, a year older'n Jefferson Neely?"

"Yup," Henry agreed. "Twenty. Determined to make his fortune. Was out in Texas before and came home. Now he's down by the crossing, readying himself for the return trip."

"Maybe he'll come with us," I suggested.

"Pa isn't likely to ask him along," Jake muttered. "Sure wish he'd bring the wagon up here. Won't happen. Grab that skillet lid, Jer, and come on. We'll have ourselves a few trips bringing these supplies down."

"I got work myself," Henry said, pushing a straw hat back from his forehead. "Good luck on the road. Hear the robbers are fierce out Arkansas way."

"Why, they'd never have a chance with me and Jericho on watch," Jake boasted. "You know he wakes at the snap of a twig?"

"Never worried over twigs," Henry said, smiling. "Just pistol balls."

Jake heaved a twenty-pound sack of flour onto one

shoulder, and I wrapped both hands around the skillet lid. Then we marched down to the wagon.

"You'll be all morning bringing down those supplies like that," Pa complained when we arrived, winded and aching. "Each of you grab one end of the box and haul it down."

"Pa, there's eighty pounds of flour up there," Jake objected. "Other stuff besides. Now how's Jericho going to lift half of that? Last time he stepped onto the grain scales in town he didn't weigh seventy pounds."

"Well, he ought to eat more," Pa grumbled. "And get some growth. Time all you boys stretched yourselves some. Living out in the open's sure to help. Toughens a man."

Me, I didn't feel much manliness coming on me that morning, but it wasn't doing us any good talking to Pa. Jake motioned me along as he set off toward the store again. Although we tried to carry the supply box, we weren't either one of us up to the task. Finally we figured out a way to roll it, putting round logs under the box. As the supplies moved along, I'd pick up the logs left behind and move them around in front. It worked well enough, but Pa was put out we hadn't done it like he'd told us.

"Next time I'll send Jane Mary and your ma," he grumbled.

"No pleasing some folks," Jake declared as he pulled me toward the wagon. We busied ourselves storing the goods until Ma called us to breakfast.

We had one surprise in store for us. As we gripped

hands and waited for Ma to say grace, she introduced us to Eli Grady.

"You're Henry's cousin," I remarked, and he grinned. Eli was thin and scarce five and a half feet tall. I figured Pa couldn't be happy at having another puny fellow around. Eli had a sort of contagious grin, though, and his dark brown eyes had a glitter to them. He was dark-haired like Henry, but paler of complexion.

"Eli's riding along with us to Texas," Ma explained, and I felt my jaw drop. Jake was just as surprised.

"Eli's bound for Wise County, just west of where your Uncle Dan's picked out our farm," Pa told us. "He's got that fine bay mare there to ride, and he's agreed to share expenses."

Now it made sense. Pa never let a chance to come by a few dollars slip past.

Eli shook our hands and expressed his gratitude for coming along. Ma put an end to that by dishing out ham and eggs. Soon enough we occupied ourselves eating breakfast.

Afterward Jane Mary took the plates down to the river and washed 'em while I helped Pa get the Morgans lined up.

"That's Bob on the left there," Josh told me as Pa slipped the harness in place. "Andy's on the right."

"Belinda and Amy are the ones in back," Jordy added.

Sandy barked as if to agree to the names, and Jake had a laughing fit.

"Hope Belinda Cromwell never hears you named a

draft horse after her," Jake declared. "Is some resemblance, I'll admit. Especially from the back."

"See, I told you," Jordy told Josh. "And you thought she was more like Miz Miranda Hopkins."

I couldn't keep myself from laughing.

"There's work needs doing!" Pa shouted, and I turned back to the horses. Jane Mary returned with the plates, and Jake tied Cathy the cow to the back of the wagon. Then, with Eli leading the way, we started toward the river.

The Tennessee River makes a sort of snakish curl through the state. In the east it runs south before bending into Alabama and Mississippi. Finally it turns north and heads up into Tennessee again, hits Kentucky, and empties into the Ohio River. All that bending makes it shallow and slow in places, and one such was at Edding's Ford.

We splashed into the river just fine, and all went well at first. Then it got deeper and deeper. Jake pulled Josh up onto the roan behind him, and Jordy climbed up behind Eli. Jane Mary sat in the back of the wagon, making faces at me. I knew what was on her mind. There I was, walking beside ole Red, Jake's horse. Me, who wasn't all that comfortable in deep water, and like as not would drown if the current took it into its head to sweep me into a hole.

Sure enough it happened. Well, I slipped anyway. Down I went, thrashing and yelling. Eli sloshed his way over and tossed me a rope. He then dragged me, sopping wet, to the far bank.

"I tell you, Jer, best work on your swimming!" Jake scolded when he and Josh joined us.

"Maybe Sandy can teach you," Jane Mary cackled.

"Hush!" Ma urged.

"Well, just look at him!" Jane Mary exclaimed. "He's soaked to the skin. Likely we'll be half the morning waiting for him to dry."

"No, we've got to climb Cumberland Mountain to-day," Pa argued, pointing at the broad slope dead ahead. "Jake, you bring him along once his clothes dry."

"We're all of us wet, Pa," Jake noted, helping Josh down.

"Get a fire built and dry yourselves," Ma ordered. "Then hurry along. You youngsters are more than a match for these horses, I'd say."

"Yes, ma'am," Jake assured her as he dismounted. Jordy jumped down from the bay, and Eli waved his farewell.

"Believe I'll let the sun dry my boots," he explained. "I don't like the look in your eyes, Jake. Mischief's afoot, I'd judge."

Jake just grinned.

Once the wagon was out of sight, he led us into a thicket. We peeled off our clothes and built a fire. But once the clothes and ourselves were dried out, Jake led us on a wild march along the river. There was plenty of pranking and a tale or two. Finally, though, Jordy complained he was hungry, and we noticed it was clos-ing in on midday. We started on a fair trot up the dusty road, covering the five miles or so we'd fallen back in no more than a good hour.

"You boys appear out of breath," Pa observed when we rejoined them. "Must have had a time getting that fire built, huh, Jake?"

"Yes, sir," Jake admitted. "Flint got wet, too."

Pa scowled some, but I could tell inside he was laughing. To hear Ma tell it, he was a rascal himself in his younger days.

We satisfied our hunger by chewing on cold ham and biscuits. All the while the wagon kept up its steady pace. It was on climbs like the one up Cumberland Mountain that we grew to appreciate the Morgans. Once in a while we'd pass another wagon stopped because its team had played out. Mules managed somewhat better, but that ridge even gave oxen a trial. Our Morgans plodded on like they were on a Sunday hayride.

By Pa's map, we covered more than ten miles that day. He wrote as much in the little black diary he'd bought at the Edding Store. We made camp atop the mountain, where the trail was narrow and treacherous. A family named Riley lived there, and they came along for a visit after supper.

"You're welcome to fill your barrel from our well," Mrs. Riley told Ma. "Bring the children along up to the house. My own are grown and gone, and I miss their voices."

"Got a hand can play the fiddle," Mr. Riley added. "If

you've a mind, you can dance to the music or else sing along. My girls always liked that."

"We'd enjoy the music, Mr. Riley," Ma told them. And indeed we did.

The fiddler was a tall black man named Franklin. I guess he was a slave, since most black people in Tennessee were back then. He didn't seem like the ones that drove grain wagons along the river, though. They always looked down at the ground and frowned a lot.

"It's the music in him," Jake declared. "Look at his eyes glow."

And Franklin did fill that porch with music. Why, he could fiddle you right into Paradise. Ma and Pa swung each other around like a pair of youngsters out spooning in April. Eli Grady, not to be outdone, invited Jane Mary to step out with him, and those two stomped and spun like I wouldn't have believed possible.

Later on, when the dancers wore down and Franklin fiddled himself some sad tunes, I sat beside him and tapped my fingers along on the porch boards.

"You got the music in you, too, youngster," Franklin said, waving me over. He showed me how to rest the fiddle against my chin and put the bow in my fingers. For half an hour he helped me play one tune after another.

"Thanks," I said when Pa announced it was time to head back to the wagon.

"You get yourself a fiddle one day, boy," he urged. "You got music trying to get out through them fingers. Help it escape."

"I will," I promised.

"You did halfway good with that fiddle," Jane Mary told me as we left the Riley place.

"Figure I'm good for something after all?" I asked.

"Not many things," she insisted. "Like fording rivers. But you might turn out to be worth the trouble you cause after all."

"Now that's high praise," Jake declared.

I knew he was joking, but I couldn't help thinking it was praise in a way. Or maybe it was just Jane Mary turning halfway human.

I fed Sandy a ham bone and helped Jake hang up the food in a game bag before hurrying to my blankets. It was turning colder, and I wasted no time settling into bed. Josh rolled over beside me again, but Jake dragged his bed a foot or so away.

"You little boys give me some room," he grumbled.

Sandy crawled over and lay down in the empty spot, and I felt the dog's hot breath on my neck.

"Good boy," I said, rubbing his nose. Then, in spite of a chorus of crickets and the sounds of animals prowling the brush, I closed my eyes and drifted off to sleep.

That night my dreams filled with fiddle playing and dancing. I imagined a hundred high times. And I didn't wake once.

CHAPTER FOUR

WE MADE ANOTHER TEN MILES ON SATURDAY. I WAS BEGIN-
ning to get used to Pa's driving us, and my feet had settled into my new boots some. I admit I grumbled at all
the trail chores I was handed, but then so did Jake,
Jordy, and Josh. To Jane Mary's credit, she ignored our
mutterings and busied herself fussing over Eli Grady.

"Poor fellow's doomed," Jake declared. "Trapped by
a female web. There's no escaping that, little brothers."

The trail down Cumberland Mountain was none too
good, but we had no mishaps. Moreover, Sandy scared
up a pair of rabbits, and Jake shot 'em dead. Fresh
meat—even rabbit—eased the strain on Pa's pocket-
book, and he almost smiled when Jake brought Ma the
rabbits.

"A nice buck would be all the more welcome," Pa said, and Jake kept his rifle tied to the back of Red's saddle afterward, hoping to come across deer tracks.

We made camp along the trail Saturday night and kept to ourselves. There were some farmers a quarter mile or so away, but they didn't seem too interested in us.

"They see lots of travelers," Eli explained. "Likely we don't concern them much. They've got trouble enough scratching out a living on this mountain."

Sunday found us still on Cumberland Mountain. That fool ridge seemed to have no end! I confess the distant view of green hills and tall trees awaiting us stirred my insides. It was as beautiful a place as I'd ever seen. Even so, I was eager to cut down the miles remaining between us and Texas.

"Collect the horses!" Pa hollered as Jake and I built up the morning cook fire. "Let's get ourselves a good start for once."

"Joe Wetherby!" Ma howled. "You don't mean to travel on the Sabbath!"

"God understands the needs of pilgrims," Pa argued. "And that's what we are, after all."

"You invite His wrath!" Ma countered. "Many's the time misfortune has befallen the wicked. You recall what happened to Amos Hadnot last Easter."

That was a famous story indeed! Amos Hadnot fell off his horse and broke both legs. As I heard it, he was getting ready to race that horse against Judge Harvey's big black stud. Ma deemed it God's judgment, but Pa

41

liked to argue it was more on account of Amos Hadnot being eighty-four years old and half blind than from any divine purpose.

I wasn't so sure. I'd known my share of boys to come down with fevers after pranking neighbors or swearing in public. My rule was, Don't try to understand such mysteries. Just leave 'em be.

"You'll have to content yourself with some Bible reading," Pa told Ma. "And prayer, of course."

"Well, I'm glad we haven't turned altogether heathen," she muttered.

As it turned out, we had time for a lot of Bible reading. Eli's bay came down with the colic, and Pa told us to leave off harnessing the Morgans.

"That horse sounds real sickly," Pa said as he looked the animal over. "Was the river crossing most likely."

"I'd judge it so," Eli agreed.

"Jericho, crawl into the wagon and fetch my turpentine," Pa instructed, and I did just that. While Pa went on examining the bay, I rummaged around until I found a half-empty bottle of spirits of turpentine. That stuff smelled bad as brimstone, and it would near take the hide off you as fast as it would peel old paint off a barn. It was Pa's favorite cure, though, and I brought the bottle to him.

He dabbed some with a cloth and took to rubbing the poor horse with it. The bay jumped and fought at first, but then calmed down after a bit. And the colic flowed right out of it.

"Well, I'll be!" Eli remarked. "Farmer, carpenter, and now horse doc. Anything you don't do, Joe?"

"Sure," Pa answered. "Get myself onto a trail when I intend to."

Ma was put out by the fast way Pa hurried everybody through breakfast, and she was downright mad about him harnessing the horses while she read her verses.

"You tempt Providence, Joe Wetherby," she warned again and again.

But Pa was more concerned with getting down Cumberland Mountain.

The trail down the west slope had been narrow and tricky from the first. It only got worse. For one thing a light drizzle took up, and I found myself sliding along in the mud, fighting to keep from slipping off the side of the ridge. There was also the danger of falling under a wagon wheel or getting stomped on by one of the Morgans.

"What a day to find myself afoot!" Jake complained. Eli's bay was tied behind the wagon, for Pa thought it best to rest a sick horse. So Eli led the way atop Red, and Jake plodded along with the rest of us boys.

"The wages of sin," Jane Mary chided us from the back of the wagon.

If there'd been a rock handy, I would've brained her proper!

Then the north wind took up its tormenting. Before long we were lashed by rain and pelted by hailstones.

"Come on back behind the wagon," Jake urged as Jordy and I pried Josh from the boggy trail. "It'll break the wind some."

Wouldn't you know it? The wind just circled around and came at us from behind!

"The Lord's judgment!" Ma hollered as the canvas wagon-cover flapped wildly.

Me, I didn't know whether it was God's wrath or just Tennessee weather. It was about the worst day I spent in my whole life. By noon I was dragging twenty pounds of mud along, not to mention Jordy. Jake was hauling Josh, and half the time the four of us were one giant ball of muck and misery.

"Know any verses?" Jordy whispered when the sky turned even uglier. It got so dark we could barely see the wagon! And we boys didn't dare close our eyes for fear we'd disappear from sight.

Sandy proved his worth that day, for he raced alongside us, yelping and urging us onward. Of course he'd been better named Blackie, with all the mud he'd taken aboard, but that dog was a cheerful sight just the same.

Was then that the sky overhead exploded. A bolt of lightning burned its way along the mountain, scorching treetops. Thunder shook the ground and upset the horses. It was Sandy's turn to go coward, for that poor collie dog hugged my leg in terror. Jordy clawed my side, and Josh took to whimpering.

Ma was scared, too, for she took up hymn singing. It was a sure sign, for she did it whenever she sensed approaching doom. Pa and Jane Mary joined in, and I was half of a mind to add my feeble voice. Jake, on the other hand, took to laughing. He sang some, too, but his ditty wasn't one you'd hear at a camp meeting. No, sir! It was all about a yellow-haired gal named Sue.

I couldn't help laughing in spite of the thunder booming out all around us. And pretty soon Josh and Jordy were singing along.

"Stop that!" Ma hollered. "It's the devil tempting you!"

Maybe it was, too, because when we stopped, the storm began to break up. By late afternoon we were sloshing along in sunlight again.

I've seen wild sights before, but I confess our camp that night put 'em all to shame. We had lines strung every place imaginable. Every inch of clothing was hung up, and a passerby would have thought himself viewing a whole town on wash day.

Jake and I built a nest of sorts—mostly sticks and the driest of the leaves we could find—up the hill a ways, and after supper we spread out three blankets we'd halfway dried over the fire. Eli lay down under one, Jake and I took the second, and Jordy and Josh crawled under the other. We were all of us stark naked on account of hanging up even our shirts to dry. Of course you'd never have known, caked in mud like we were.

Miserable as that day had been, the night was even

worse. It turned downright cold, and I shivered the whole time. Jake finally had to pull Josh over and shake him awake.

"Stop that whimpering!" Jake commanded. "Won't any of us get any rest!"

"I'm frozen, Jake," Josh complained.

Jake just laughed and told us an old Daniel Boone tale. When that didn't chase off the gloom, he invented a story about the mud people. Wasn't hard to imagine those folks, gazing around at Eli and my brothers. Afterward, we built ourselves a fire and huddled close to the warmth.

"You know what Pa thinks about burning fires at night," Jordy said, easing his mud creature feet closer. "We might just burn up this whole mountainside."

"No chance," Eli declared as he let Josh's head slide down onto one knee. "I won't be getting any sleep this night."

"Me, neither," Jordy admitted. "I'm frozen."

"Besides," I added, "mud creatures aren't afraid of fire, are they, Jake?"

"Not afraid of anything," he announced. "Except maybe sisters."

We laughed as he told about the wicked brown-haired demon who took after the mud creatures with a skillet lid. I wager we all of us pictured Jane Mary's vengeful eyes and sharp tongue. When the tale concluded, I curled up beside the fire and drifted off into a light sleep.

Nobody had to rouse us that next morning. No sooner had our fire died out than the whole batch of us took to shivering. I was wide awake, with every stitch of clothes I owned on me, a long time before the sun topped the horizon. For once Jake had a fire blazing before Pa had a chance to holler about it.

"You boys appear to be getting used to the road," Pa said instead. "I like to see youngsters take to the challenges of a journey."

I was struck dumb. Jordy and Josh were still thawing out their toes. Jake wasn't one to miss a chance at praise, though.

"We'll try to measure up, Pa," he announced, scratching his ear. " 'Course you got to realize we didn't have any critters to fight last night and no dancing to wear us down."

"Think that's where the fault lies, eh?" Pa asked.

"Could be," Jake said, managing his best grin. "And don't forget. Jer near wore himself to a nub playing the fiddle Friday night."

"Well, that's behind him now," Pa observed. "Since you're so full of fire this morn, Jake, why don't you start hitching the Morgans. We could do with an early start for once."

"No horses to tonic?" Jake asked.

"Not this time," Eli said as he led his bay past the wagon. "Took to the cure, it seems."

"I'll keep some spirits of turpentine ready just the same," Pa declared. "A colic can come back on you."

While Pa and Eli discussed horse doctoring, Jake and I saw to the Morgans. By that time Ma and Jane Mary had started on breakfast, and the aroma of sizzling ham slices and popping eggs had my hollow innards rumbling with hunger. I could scarce work fast enough so we could hurry back to camp and eat.

"Wait just a minute there, Jericho Wetherby!" Ma shouted when I trotted over and grabbed a plate.

"Yes, ma'am?" I asked.

"You don't expect to come to table without washing, do you?" she demanded.

"Table?" I asked, gazing around me in bewilderment.

"Just a figure of speech," she barked. "There's a basin of water yonder. Wash your face and hands. Hear?"

"Yes, ma'am," I mumbled as I turned and did as ordered. My sole comfort lay in knowing Ma wouldn't say grace before everybody was collected, and no one dared eat before the blessing. Even so, I felt sure I'd starve before I scraped the mud off me and joined the others. Ma made special mention of her muddy boys in the prayer and requested better traveling weather. She must have had the Lord's ear, for the sun burned off a low fog and spread a welcome warmth across the land.

Monday proved to be our best day yet, and we rolled along more than ten miles. It turned cool again that night, but we had dry clothes and blankets to warm us, and Eli showed us how to make a nest of oak and willow leaves to fend off the ground chill. I was limp as an old moccasin when I pulled my blanket

against my chin. With Sandy lying on my feet, Josh and Jordy squished in-between Jake and me, and a fire crackling nearby, I was real close to contentment.

Tuesday dawned even brighter. We were up and at our chores early again, so I suppose Pa was right to say we were growing accustomed to travel. Me, I'd have been happy to stay in one place from time to time, but I knew winter was chasing us to Texas.

"Can't let the snows catch us in the wilds," Eli warned at breakfast. "Miserable hard going, trudging along through the ice, with a wind biting at your ribs."

I shuddered just to imagine it. I was cold enough coming down Cumberland Mountain!

Jordy and I scraped the plates that morning while Jake and Pa got the wagon packed up. We ended up on the trail earlier than ever, and we maintained a steady pace most of the day. Now that we were past the rough country around Cumberland Mountain, the road was considerably better. We soon found out why, for a fellow had built himself a rail fence across the road. There was a little shack alongside, too.

"Toll gate," Eli announced. "The price of progress."

"What's that?" Jordy asked.

"Well, nobody's much interested in building roads so folks can cross their fields," Eli explained. "When a fellow does, he puts up a gate and gets his investment back by charging tolls."

"It's the same as Jackson's Ferry on the Knoxville road," Jake added. "Many of 'em, Eli?"

"More every year," Eli grumbled. "I hear it's down-right expensive crossing Arkansas."

It wasn't cheap traveling Tennessee. That fellow at the toll gate held us up for a whole silver dollar, which was close to criminal seeing how the road was rutted and puddled from the gate all the way to Sparta. We boys were muddy enough already, and being splattered with muck for fifteen more miles, we could have passed for chocolate cake.

"We'll be stopping awhile in Sparta, Mary Elizabeth," Pa told Ma late that afternoon. "We'll want to buy a few things, and I want to change some of my Knoxville bank notes into gold and silver. Eli says folks look with suspicion on paper money west of Nashville."

"But we're not going to Nashville," Ma argued. "And I dislike having a lot of coinage about. Attracts thieves."

"We have to adapt to the custom, dear," Pa insisted. "It may be even worse in Texas."

"Then I suppose it's for the best," she said, sighing. "My own family has never trusted bank paper, so I guess it's unfair to expect otherwise of these folks. Still, it's worrisome."

But banks weren't much concern to a twelve-year-old. Or so I thought. When we got to Sparta, Ma took a good look at us boys and insisted on a detour to a nearby spring.

"This is a proper town," she cried. "And here you boys look like river tramps. What will people think?"

"Likely they'll figure we've been through some mud," Jordy said.

"It's been raining, Ma," Jake added. "Won't be many surprised we're a hair rough-looking."

"Lots of families pass through Sparta," Eli said. "I don't imagine anybody will take notice."

"The quality folk will," Ma argued. "And I won't have my family spoken of as low-account vagabonds!"

"We have to pass through Sparta," Pa complained. "I have to change these notes, and . . ."

"Go ahead, Joe," Ma suggested. "I'll remain here at the spring and see these boys get a thorough scrubbing."

"Ma?" Jordy exclaimed. "We can't take a bath out here. There's people about."

"Never much bothered you down at the river," Jane Mary said, laughing. "Who'd take note of you, Jordy?"

"There's females yonder!" Jordy said, pointing to a collection of women filling barrels at the spring.

"We'll put up a pair of blankets on a line," Ma announced. "Now stop your fussing. We'll need to fill buckets first. Then you'd better start washing. Unless you would like Jane Mary to do it for you."

"No, ma'am," Josh said, shrinking from Ma's annoyed gaze.

"Do it proper, too!" Ma added. "Jake, you see to it."

"I was hoping to go with Pa," Jake objected.

"You're as dirty as your brothers," Ma observed. "Now, watch yourselves, Joe, Eli. I'll be along in the wagon once I get these boys started on their bath."

"Don't dawdle, you four," Pa warned. "Get washed quick and come along to town."

"Can't drag all these buckets and blankets," Jake argued.

"You'd best leave the wagon, Mary Elizabeth," Pa suggested. "Jake can drive it in, and you can ride his horse."

"I'll have no dealings with horses," Ma muttered. "I'll walk."

"I'll ride," Jane Mary declared.

"You'll walk with your mother, as befits a young lady," Ma insisted. "Jake, don't you hurry those horses. They've got miles to go yet today, and they're weary already."

"It's only half a mile," Jake muttered. "I believe I can get a wagon that far without killing any horses."

Ma didn't say anything, but she wasn't looking any too confident about things. Still, she strung up the blankets, set us to fetching water from the spring, and picked out clean clothes for the trip to town.

"Now I mean what I say about you scrubbing yourselves," she said before leaving. "If I spy one speck of mud behind an ear, I'm just liable to finish the job myself, then and there, even if it means stripping you bare on Main Street!"

Now that would sure make for a memorable visit to Sparta! Nobody'd soon forget the Wetherbys then.

"Figure she means that?" Jordy asked after she grabbed Jane Mary and started for Sparta.

"No," I told him. "But she'd turn you over to Jane Mary, and that'd be near as bad."

"Worse," Josh declared. "Jane Mary gave me a bath once, and I couldn't walk proper for a week after."

Josh made a face, winced in pretended pain, and we all laughed. Then Jake decided it was time to get to the subject at hand, and we started stripping. I've had baths in rivers and tubs, but that was my first spring-water bucket wash. It wasn't something I'd wish on an enemy. No, sir. To get the mud off took considerable effort and powerful soap. The lye burned, and the wind whipped up and near froze the exposed parts of us. We were scrubbing and shivering and doing a fair portion of grumbling, and about the best thing we could any of us say was that we got it done in half an hour and dressed ourselves.

We were none of us altogether clean, but when goose bumps grow the size of walnuts, you figure surviving's got its limits. Jake satisfied himself our ears and faces were free of dirt, and we cleaned out our fingernails and gave every hand an extra wash.

"I guess we'll pass muster," Jake finally declared. "Let's get the buckets emptied, the blankets taken down, and this wagon rolling on to Sparta."

"You got yourself a deal!" I shouted, and Jordy and Josh added a whoop of their own. We got it done in short order, and Jake tied his horse behind the wagon, climbed up top, and took the lines.

"Hop aboard, Wetherbys," he hollered. "This wagon's headed out."

We piled in back with the supplies, and Jake poked the Morgans into motion. Wasn't any time before we were rumbling down the rutted road to Sparta.

CHAPTER FIVE

To be truthful, Sparta wasn't worth a bath. If you blinked, you were liable to miss the whole town! Pa did swap some of his bank notes for double eagles—twenty-dollar gold pieces—but it wasn't an even-up trade. Bankers didn't favor Knoxville banks, and they only valued those notes at ninety cents on the dollar.

"I expected better of Tennesseans," Pa grumbled afterward. The shopkeepers turned up their noses at folding money, though, and a farmer warned us the folks down the road wouldn't take notes, either.

"Been some banks go bust, I expect," Pa told us.

"That's not it," Jake said, laughing. "Most of these farmers and traders can't read. They can recognize coins by color and size, but they wouldn't know a twenty-dollar bank note from a newspaper."

"Jake!" Pa scolded.

"Just repeating what I heard over at the bank," Jake explained. "Fellow said if you've got bank notes left, best exchange 'em in Memphis. Folks in Arkansas make Tennessee farmers seem pure educated."

"I won't abide such talk," Pa objected. "We'll find them good, God-fearing folk, I'm certain. If they've not had the benefits of learning, it's not likely their doing. Now get your horse, boy, and let's collect the women. There are miles we can still travel today."

Ma and Jane Mary were chatting with a couple of town ladies, and prying them loose was worse than pulling a muskrat out of a bear trap. The trail was mighty short of female company, and Ma was in no hurry to climb back onto the wagon and bounce along westward.

"We'll just be a little longer," Ma said when Jake and I explained Pa was ready to leave. "Don't you have supplies to buy?"

"Not at their prices," Jake answered. "Rascal wants a dollar for a bushel of corn!"

"That rascal's my husband, young man!" one of the ladies stormed.

"Tell him his corn's high," Jake said, matching the woman's hard stare. "We're only pilgrims, traveling to the promised land."

"Before you get much farther, you may recall Sparta as an oasis of kindness," the woman countered. "Winter's coming, and not everyone will spare food for any price."

The lady appeared serious, and I wondered if it wouldn't be wise to stock up on cornmeal when the chance happened along. I wasn't deciding things, of course, so my thoughts weren't much use to anybody. Ma waved Jake and me along, then said her good-byes. Once we were clear of town, she read Jake a verse or two about respecting elders.

"Oh, Ma, the whole town skins travelers," Jake complained. "I heard that road isn't even a real pike. Fellow just put himself up a rail across the road and charges folks."

"Happens sometimes," Eli told us. "But I didn't notice people in Sparta being all that hard. You got to expect a man to try and make a profit."

"I do," Pa replied. "But double the going price would appear a hair unreasonable."

Sandy barked sharply as if to agree, and I figured the matter settled. It wasn't. Jake, Eli, and Pa argued another hour after we rolled out of Sparta. I dropped behind with Jordy and Josh, and we took turns tossing Sandy sticks to fetch. If some people just had as much good sense as dogs, there'd be a whole lot less arguing and more stick-fetching.

We crossed another six or seven miles before Pa judged the Morgans tired. That southern stretch of White County was mostly farms, and people seemed poor. Little children were barefooted, even in October, and their clothes were pitiful ragged. Even so, whole families hurried down to the road to wave us a howdy-do, and toward dusk one batch, the Cokes, invited us to camp near their house.

"Wouldn't want to put you folks to any trouble," Pa said.

"Why not?" Mr. Coke asked. "It's my trouble, isn't it? You wouldn't want to camp on the road. We've had some people bothered lately down near the river. Too many idle hands about, if you ask me."

"Idle hands do the devil's biddin'," Mrs. Coke noted.

"Not much chance of the devil findin' help hereabouts," a lanky boy about my age grumbled. "Near enough work to bend a boy over double."

"Now, Billy, you hush that talk," Mrs. Coke said. Her face betrayed a grin, though, and Billy gave her a quick "yes'm" as he brushed a handful of unruly straw-colored hair from his eyes.

"Billy and me got ourselves a deer night 'fore last," Mr. Coke announced. "We'd have you share our table if you've a mind. Just smoked venison and greens's all, but it satisfies."

"Ma could cook skunk so you'd find it tasty," Billy declared.

"Stop that braggin' now," his mother barked, turning her head away.

"You can take your horses around back," Mr. Coke told Pa. "Looks to storm tonight, so it's best to hobble 'em. Wish I could offer you a bed, but we've just got our one. The youngsters spread out beside the fire.

You're welcome to make yourselves at home in the barn, though. Roof won't leak, and there's straw to lay on."

"Be high living after Cumberland Mountain," Eli said, grinning at Jane Mary. "Maybe I can help chop you some stove wood?"

"Always in need of it," Mrs. Coke admitted. "Billy, you show this young fella where to find an ax. Then pump us some water."

"Chores," Billy muttered.

"You'll have time to visit later," Mr. Coke said, lifting the boy's chin. "Now hurry along."

We settled in at the Coke place like long-lost kin. Jake and I freed the Morgans from their harness and led them past the barn to a watering trough. Billy brought two dozen binds of fodder from the barn, and the horses started in on it.

"That your dog?" Billy asked as Sandy trotted over.

"Yup," I told him. "My grandpa gave him to me. Sandy's a better companion than a couple of little brothers."

"Sure," Billy agreed. "I got some hounds. My Uncle Sime's got 'em off scarin' up coons most likely. Can't complain as he's taken two brothers along."

"Wondered if it was just you," I said, giving Sandy an ear scratch.

"No, there's eight of us boys and three girls," Billy explained. "Others's doin' chores. Got an older sister, Ruth, besides that. She works for a woman up 'round

Franklin. Once my bitty brothers get some size, Pa's sure to hire me off, too."

"Don't know I'd like that," I said, shaking my head. "There's a time or two when I've had all the family I figure to ever need, but it's good to have kin when the hard times come."

"Hereabouts, that's most always," Billy said, stroking Sandy's back. "But I expect I'll miss Ma's cookin'."

That evening I found out why. Billy wasn't boasting about his mother. Mrs. Coke put together a regular feast of venison steaks, collard greens, lima beans, and corn muffins, all topped off with an apple pie that made me forget my weariness. After dinner Eli and Jane Mary volunteered to scrape the plates. Jake and I hobbled the horses and moved our blankets into the barn. Wasn't half an hour later the ground began shaking, and giant hailstones started whipping around the house like musket balls.

"Told you there appeared to be a storm comin'," Mr. Coke reminded us.

"We'll be glad of a roof this night," Eli declared. "Not fond of listening to Jordy's teeth chattering and Jericho's ribs playing a tune."

"My ribs don't play any tunes," I argued.

"Then I guess it must be pure, old-fashioned snoring I keep hearing," Eli said, poking my side. "Hard to believe anybody so skinny could make such a racket!"

"I'm not that skinny," I complained.

"Well, if you was to be a deer, you'd be safe from a

rifle," Billy told me. "Fella'd starve for sure dependin' on your meat to see him through the winter."

"I don't know," Jake said, laughing. "We ate that coon."

"Well, we'd never be hungry enough to cook up Jericho," Jane Mary insisted. "Give us all bellyache."

"Nice to know I'd be remembered," I said sourly.

"We'd never eat you, Jer," Josh said, grinning. "Ma doesn't take with cannibals and such."

"He's right," Jake agreed. "So I guess you're safe, little brother."

I'd had enough of such talk, so I slipped out the door and huddled with Sandy on the porch. The poor dog was cold and soggy, and he eagerly curled up beside me. That wasn't any comfort for me, but gazing at the storm, I said a prayer or two of thanks for the Cokes' hospitality. That night, nesting in the straw while rain hammered on the roof overhead, I was even gladder. It turned cold later on, and I woke up sandwiched between Jake and Jordy, with Sandy sprawled across our legs.

"Glad the weather's turned warm," Jake whispered when he noticed my open eyes. "I feel half frozen."

"Only half?" I asked.

He laughed and elbowed my side, urging, "Get some more rest, Jer. We got a river to cross this day."

I felt myself grow weary all over just thinking of it.

Wednesday proved to be a trial from the first. The weather was nasty cold, with misty rain falling the whole time. The horses had managed to stray, and Jake and I had a busy morning finding them. Then we had to give them a good rub. Meanwhile Pa and Eli were busy pulling the left back wheel off the wagon.

"Got a couple of bad spokes," Mr. Coke observed when we stared at the wagon. "We'll shave an oak branch or two and make replacements."

"That'll take all morning," Pa muttered. "So there's no need to harness the team just yet."

"Yes, sir," I said, gazing nervously at Jake.

"Come on," he suggested. "We'll help roll up blankets. Pa won't be in any mood for company till we're back on the road."

I nodded my agreement and trotted along.

Jake was sure right about Pa. Truth is, between the foul weather and the late start, he was downright rankled. He had the Morgans breathing hard after five miles, and we walkers were strung out a quarter mile back, hoping to avoid mud-spattering wheels and fatherly rebukes.

We didn't find much to celebrate at the Rock Island Ferry, either. The Caney Fork River, as it was called, had swollen with runoff, and there was no wading across. We had to pay to ferry the wagon, the horses, and all us humans, too. Jake volunteered to swim, until he dipped a toe in the water. It was colder than December ice. The ferry fellow made a good profit off the Wetherbys. Our only bargain was Sandy.

"The dog can come along free," the ferryman declared. "I'm partial to collies."

We got across Caney Fork River with only one scare. That wobbly ferry caught itself once in the current and strained at its lines.

"Once saw a ferry break loose up in Virginia," the ferry fellow recounted. "Drowned twenty people."

"Hush, Daniel!" his partner shouted. "You'll scare off business."

Or drown it, I was thinking. Anyway, we got to the other side in fine shape and resumed the journey west.

We were fortunate enough to find another friendly farm family that night. The Talbots charged us for cornmeal and fodder, but they offered us their barn, and Mrs. Talbot baked up a cherry cobbler just for us youngsters.

"Had six children myself," the little gray-haired woman told us. "Oldest lived to see his sixth birthday. This here's hard-hearted country! Swallows young 'uns and leaves their grievin' mas to live on."

We all made a fuss over the cobbler, which didn't turn out to taste near as good as it looked, and that brightened Miz Talbot some. The story turned Ma to thinking on the twins, though, and I heard her crying some that night.

Next day, after passing another cold night huddled in straw with my brothers, we packed up the wagon, harnessed the team, and rolled on toward McMinnville. It was cold and foggy, but the road was wide and a bit drier. The only trouble came at Rolling River. There was no ferry, and the river cut a deep gash in the country. Somebody had built a bridge, but it was too narrow for wagons.

"We'll have to take the wagon downstream and find a ford," Eli announced. "No point everybody getting wet, though. I'll drive the wagon. Take care of my horse, Jake."

"Sure," Jake agreed as he accepted the reins. Jane Mary and Ma climbed down with us boys, and Jake nudged his horse toward the bridge.

"Best we lead the horses, son," Pa advised. "Animals can turn skittish, and you wouldn't want to be thrown off this bridge."

"Not this one," Jake agreed. "No, sir."

Up to then I hadn't taken a real good look at that bridge. When I did, I gasped. The thing was just warped planks bound together with odd pieces of twine, and the river was close to forty feet down, with jagged rocks all around.

"Maybe I ought to go with Eli," I suggested.

"Eli can drive a wagon," Pa replied. "You'd just slow him down. Jake, bring the horses. Jericho, bring your brothers along."

"Yes, sir," I said. But my feet didn't manage even a hint of movement.

"It's mighty high up, huh?" Jordy whispered.

"Long way down," Josh observed.

"Come on," Jake called from up ahead. "Won't get any easier."

"Here," I suggested, offering Jordy my hand. "We'll do it together."

"Not me," Jordy said, shaking his head.

"Oh, it's not so much," Josh said, watching Pa cross to the far side. "Ma and Jane Mary have gone and done it."

He took a deep breath then and scrambled after Jake. Sandy barked at me, and I nodded. The fool collie trotted along with Josh, leaving only Jordy and me, the Wetherby cowards, behind.

"I never knew heights to do a fellow much good," Jordy said, shuddering. "You scared, too, Jer?"

"Not me," I lied, forcing myself toward the bridge.

"No, I'm just sweating like a plow horse," Jordy declared.

"Come on, boys!" Pa bellowed.

"It's too high," Jordy whimpered.

"Can't live the rest of our lives here," I said, gripping his wrist tightly. "Close your eyes, Jordy, and follow along. Only don't look down."

"Don't worry on that account," he assured me.

Looking back on it, I don't suppose that bridge was more than forty feet long. It seemed more like forty miles to Jordy and me, though. We got a quarter of the way across all right. Then Jordy peeked over the side. He shook, and I pulled him closer. I tried not to look myself, but I did, and that about finished us. I might as well have been walking on air. That bridge was creaking and groaning, and I could see the knots loosening up right before my eyes. I prayed some angel from heaven would fly us over to the far side, but angels being busy, Jake came instead.

"Grab hold of my arm," he told me.

"I can't move," I whimpered.

"Come on," he said, rubbing my shoulder and steadying my nerves. "This isn't half as high as that fool Cumberland Mountain. And not near as dangerous as fighting that bear on the Tennessee River."

"It was a coon," I said, laughing as I remembered.

"Might've been a bear," Jake said, pulling me along. Jordy stumbled on behind, and as Jake recounted other Wetherby adventures, the bridge seemed to sturdy itself up. Now our feet were moving, it wasn't so hard to keep them going. We settled into a tempo of sorts, and the next thing I knew, we were across.

"Told you it wasn't so much," Josh yelled.

"Was enough," Jordy said, leaning on my side and letting the air flow out of his lungs.

"Yup," I agreed. "Plenty enough."

CHAPTER SIX

WE MET ELI AND THE WAGON A MILE OR SO UP THE TRAIL, and by midmorning we'd rolled into McMinnville, seat of Warren County. Pa quickly deemed the place more to his liking. The prices were reasonable, for one thing. We bought eleven pounds of sugar for a dollar, and Pa picked himself up a bottle of cordial for ten cents.

McMinnville was a quarry town, and we passed wagons carting rock to Nashville or Chattanooga. Jake traded some town boys out of polished bits of stone, and I passed half an hour watching an old man carve inscriptions in grave markers.

"Here lies Abner Spence," one clever one began. "Born here, died, and left us hence."

"Made that one up myself," the carver boasted.

I might have stayed around, watching longer, but Pa was in a hurry to continue our journey, and I bid him good-bye.

"Watch that western country," the old man warned when I started on my way. "I've had a lot of work come out of there lately. Carpenter's made two dozen coffins the past two weeks."

I thought it likely a jest, but Pa said he'd heard there was typhoid fever along the Collins River. Sure enough we spied black cloth hung across porches of houses down on the river, and a wagon full of coffins passed us headed that way.

"Not much to encourage travelers," Ma observed.

"I don't know," Jake argued. "Hurries me right along. Got no hankering to take sick. Be happy when we're clear of here."

That was my feeling, too. And when we saw a second wagon of coffins, I noticed we stepped up our pace.

Beyond McMinnville, Warren County was mighty barren. Mostly the hills were timbered with blackjack oak, and we saw few fields. We did come across some monster ant beds. Jake and I measured one that was seven feet across, and when Jordy kicked it, whole regiments of ants came pouring out!

"Best we watch where we make camp tonight," Jake said. "Be a fine thing to be carted off by ants in your sleep."

"Or gnawed down to your bones," Jordy said, shuddering. "Enough of 'em to do it, don't you think, Jer?"

"Enough to eat Josh anyhow," I said, nodding my head in pretended thought. I took care to keep Sandy clear of those ants, though. I could spare a brother, but dogs were hard to come by.

We must have traveled twenty miles when Pa finally deemed the Morgans in need of rest. We'd looked for a friendly farm, but Warren County was mainly given over to ants and crows that October. We made camp at a small stream, and Ma mixed some of the sugar with some of Grandpa's peaches to make a cobbler. It was sweet enough to make us forget the salt pork and hard cornbread that preceded it.

We passed a quiet, cool night there, lying in a nest of oak leaves. For once the wind was quiet, and we didn't even miss a fire. Come morning we found our blankets and eyebrows painted with white frost, and we were a comical sight to say the least.

"What do you say, Grandpa Jer?" Jake asked me, imitating a toothless old-timer.

"What's that?" I asked, raising my hand to my ear like old Widow Lessing liked to do. "Eh? Eh?"

"Stop that, you boys!" Ma growled. "You shouldn't make fun of your elders. You'll be old yourselves one day."

"Not those two," Jane Mary objected. "Bound to be hung or shot long before any gray hairs sprout."

"Could be," Jake confessed. His eyes sparkled, and I couldn't wait to see what followed. "At least I won't be an old hen pestering and tormenting the male population. Give me a good river pirate any day over a sharp-toothed sister!"

"Ma!" Jane Mary cried.

"Be kind, Jacob," Ma scolded.

"You better be," I added. "Elsewise Jane Mary'll bake up some more of that cornbread of hers. Poison us certain."

Jordy and Josh joined in the taunts then, and Jane Mary stormed off to plan her revenge. We were all mighty relieved when Pa set us to chores. We soon had camp broken, gear stowed, and the Morgans hitched.

"Looks like we're on to Texas, Sandy," I whispered as I gave my collie a ham bone. Sandy barked his answer and gratefully accepted the bone. He gnawed it every chance he got the whole day.

Was that Friday we came across a real unusual occurrence. The trail swung west down the dry bed of Noah's Fork of Duck River, and after a mile or so of traveling that hard, caked mud, the river came bubbling up.

"Comes out of nowhere," Jake cried.

"A real oddity," Eli admitted.

Then, ten miles or so down the bed, the river went and vanished again.

"The Disappearing River," Jordy named it. "Sure is a thing to make you wonder."

"Just another Tennessee trick, if you ask me," Josh grumbled. "Lucky it didn't flood us out."

"Must be Jane Mary's prayers saved us," Eli announced. "Sure can't be any of you boys' doing."

"Jericho did some powerful praying when we crossed that bridge," Jordy pointed out. "And I did my share afterward."

"Must be what's done it," Eli said, grinning. "Good Lord loves a reformed sinner."

I sure hoped so, for our disappearing river gathered its strength and turned into a considerable stream. Worse, we were on the north bank, and the trail turned south. There was a bridge wide enough for the wagon this time, but it was higher than the other one and only half as stout. Every plank groaned and creaked, and I judged a good wind would blow the whole tottering wreck clear to New Orleans.

"You made it across the other one," Jake said, dismounting his horse. "Grab my hand, Jer. Jordy, take the other one. Now come on across, little brothers."

"It appears unsafe, Jake," I complained.

"We'll fall off and be drowned!" Jordy added.

"Hush, you two," Jake said, plopping his coonskin cap onto Jordy's head so it covered his eyes. "I just got the one cap, Jer. You figure you can manage this walk, or should I get you across one at a time?"

"Carry 'em on a cradleboard like an Indian papoose," Jane Mary suggested. "Little babies. Scared of bridges."

"Almost wouldn't mind falling off if you went, too," I told her.

"Best get accustomed to bridges, boys," Eli warned. "Be more yet to come."

I groaned, and Jordy gripped Jake's wrist with both hands.

"Remember those prayers, Jer?" Jordy whispered.

"Sure," I told him.

"Say one for me, too, will you?"

We got ourselves across through a mixture of prayer, Jake's prodding, and Jane Mary's taunts. It was a hair humiliating, being so scared of those bridges. My bitty brother Josh was running right across, and here I was, shaking myself half to death.

"Next time you boys cross on your own!" Pa barked when we stumbled off the far end.

"They did all right," Jake argued.

"Ain't fitting, being afraid like that," Pa scolded. "And fear's a thing a man conquers easier when he's young. Just builds as he gets older."

We camped beside a spring on the riverbank that night. We found a trading post there, and Pa bought fodder for the horses and half a bushel of corn. We baked up ears in the coals, and Ma roasted a pair of our chickens. It was a sort of celebration for making another twenty miles' progress, and if we'd had a fiddler, we might just have danced some.

Instead Jake and I crafted a shelter of sorts out of oak branches, and we had some cover from the frost and the wind. When we were spreading out our blankets later on, Jake took me off to one side.

"Pa's right about being afraid," he told me. "And the time may come when you have to get Jordy across."

"Don't you ever get afraid, Jake?" I asked.

"Now and then," he confessed. "But I just swallow

real hard and go ahead and do the thing. It's over soon enough."

"But I get so tied-in-knots scared. I can't even walk."

"Oh, you can walk, all right," Jake insisted. "Just put one foot down and then the other. By and by you're across."

It was easy for him to say, though. I don't believe Jake was ever real frightened of anything. No, he'd wrestle a bear and find something to laugh about even if he had an ear bit off.

Saturday we started into rough country. The road cut through limestone hills studded with beech and cedar trees, and it must have been pretty country in spring. Now the beeches were gray haunts, and their stark branches reminded me winter was coming fast. The cedars were green, as they always were, but they were stunted and scrubby.

That morning we came across a big cut in the trees, though. As far as you could see, north and south, a lane had been cleared and leveled.

"It's the Nashville Railroad," Eli said, galloping ahead and stopping beside the rails. Overhead telegraph lines were strung on tall poles, and you could occasionally hear humming sounds. I had been told you could tell trains were coming by listening to the rails, so I put my ear down and listened. I wasn't sure what you were supposed to hear, but I sort of felt a full vibration.

"Train's coming," I announced.

"Then we'd best get on across," Pa declared, waving

the wagon along. Ma poked the Morgans, and the wagon rolled over the tracks to the far side. Eli and Jake trotted past on their horses, with Josh and Jordy a step behind. I waited until I saw the distant curl of smoke on the northern horizon before leaving the rails. Then, growing cold, I glanced around for Sandy.

"There," Josh whispered, pointing back to the tracks. Somehow Sandy had managed to get one of his paws stuck between the rail and one of the ties, and he whined to me for help.

"No, Jer!" Eli yelled, but I didn't hesitate. I raced back to my dog and started working on the trapped foot. Pa, Ma, Jake, and even Jane Mary hollered at me to get clear of the tracks, but I had no ears for warnings. I could hear the train blasting its whistle, could feel the rails thrumming.

"Jer, come on!" Jake screamed.

"He's my dog!" I answered as I worked loose rock away from the tie. The train blew its whistle in short, loud, ear-piercing notes, and I knew there wasn't much time left. Out of the corner of my eye I saw the locomotive a couple of hundred yards away.

"Leave the dog!" Pa urged.

It wasn't in me, though. I could feel that paw working its way free of the trap, and I just knew I'd get it loose in another minute. Sandy was struggling and barking. I was fighting to finish the job and praying it would be in time. Then suddenly he was free. I rolled clear of the track, dragging my dog along. Wasn't seconds later the train roared past, near smothering me with grit and rock. One of the train people shouted something, and another waved an angry fist. But Sandy licked my face, and I hugged him like a long-lost friend.

When the train finally rumbled past, I stumbled over beside the wagon, shaking like a leaf in a cyclone.

"Don't you ever do something so stupid again!" Ma shouted.

"We thought you were squashed for sure, Jer," Jordy told me. "Missing an arm at least."

"Hush!" Ma hollered. I could see her eyes were reddening, and I recalled standing next to her beside the graves.

"Sorry to've worried you, Ma," I told her. "Couldn't let anything happen to Sandy, though."

"Keep a closer watch on that dog," Pa commanded. "And we'll find you some extra chores tonight for disobeying."

"Yes, sir," I said, dropping my chin onto my chest.

Later on, when we resumed the journey, Jake lifted me up behind him on his horse.

"Afraid, huh?" he whispered. "Near got yourself crushed by a train to save Sandy."

"Pretty fool-headed, I guess, Jake. But I couldn't help it."

"I know," he said. "I was a little shaky getting across that first bridge. But pulling you and Jordy over, I plumb forgot my nervousness. I'd guess you wouldn't find yourself shy of backbone when it was needed, little brother. No, you'll do."

"I take that as high praise, Jake," I said, stealing his coonskin cap.

"Tell you what," he said, taking it back. "Some night pretty soon we'll go shoot another coon, and I'll help you make your own cap. How's that sound?"

"Just fine," I said, grinning from ear to ear.

"Then it's a bargain, Jer. But don't go finding me any bears. I get a little weak-kneed around such critters."

"Not you, Jake," I argued.

"Yup, me," he said, easing me back to the ground. "But don't you go telling anybody. I'd have to hang you upside down 'neath a beehive."

"Don't you worry," I told him, my eyes widening as I imagined such a fate. "Secret's safe with me."

"Thought so," he said, riding over and pulling Jordy up behind him. I watched the two of them, figuring Jake was cheering Jordy as he had me. Was a fine thing, having Jake Wetherby for a brother. Almost balanced out Jane Mary!

We crossed Duck River again at Shelbyville, but I didn't hold on to Jake going across. The bridge wasn't as high, or didn't seem it anyway, and Jake had ridden ahead with Eli and Pa.

"Got a hand free?" Jordy asked as I stepped onto the first plank.

"Need one?" I asked.

"Might help us steady our feet," he said, shuddering as he glanced at the water sweeping by underneath.

"Might at that," I agreed, gripping his wrist. "I get a little uneasy on these fool bridges, you know."

"You?" Jordy asked. "Not after about getting run down by that train!"

"Maybe a little less," I confessed. "But they still worry me some."

"Worry me a lot," Jordy said, tightening his grip as the wagon passed by, rocking the bridge considerably.

"We'll cross 'em together from now on," I suggested. "Pure foolishness, being afraid. I know that. Still, can't seem to help it."

"No, ccccan't seemmm ttto," he stammered.

"And would you just look at Josh there," I said, watching him chase Sandy across.

"He, uh, ain't got the, uh, sense to be scared," Jordy said, forcing a grin onto his face.

"Now that's the pure truth," I agreed.

And as Jordy thought up a story to tell on Josh, he quickened his pace. We were across before you could snap your fingers. Jake was sitting atop his horse on the far side, grinning and nodding his head.

"Was his idea, walking across with me, huh?" I whispered to Jordy.

"He told me it was yours," Jordy said, gazing at me with surprise. "Big brothers can sure be a puzzle, huh?"

"Some can," I agreed. But I didn't number Jake among them.

77

CHAPTER SEVEN

IT'S FUNNY HOW JUST WHEN YOU FIGURE THINGS ARE TURN-ing for the better, they go and get worse. That next week was proof of it. First, on Sunday, the rains re-turned. Afterward the roads were fearful muddy, and we did well to manage fifteen miles a day. We didn't find much hospitality, either. There were plenty of houses and even towns along the road, but nobody in-vited us to use their well, much less pass the night in a barn or share supper.

Ma blamed the bad weather on traveling on the Sab-bath, but Pa judged it only natural for October. What-ever the cause, we had our share of trials.

First off, Pa and Eli decided to fell a giant poplar on Monday. That tree was close to eight feet across at its bottom, and we couldn't use that much firewood in a week. There's something about big trees that brings the fool out in a man, Jake said, and I have to say I agree with him. Took hours to chop through, and when it fell, it missed the wagon by less than three feet. What it did manage was to block the road. Pa and Eli were up half the night chopping that poplar into sections light enough to drag clear of the road, and if they got any sleep, it was a pure miracle.

Truth is, the rest of us didn't get many winks. A big ax crashing against a poplar in those hills makes more racket than ten locomotives, and we rose bleary-eyed and cross. Jane Mary chose that moment to start up a faultfinding crusade, and Ma agreed on most every point. Of course, we boys were the guilty ones.

I confess we hadn't devoted much time to Bible-reading or practicing ciphers, but then who had the time? We weren't idle, walking twenty miles a day, chopping firewood, tending the animals, fetching water, and such. Still, Ma insisted we study some each evening, and so Jake and I had to postpone our coon hunt.

Jane Mary's second complaint was that we weren't helping enough at mealtime. Well, I'd like to know how much cooking would get done if we weren't filling the water barrels and building the fires! Ma soon had us assigned as our sister's personal slaves, and when we weren't mixing batter or scrubbing griddles, we were listening to Jane Mary list our shortcomings.

"Red-haired boys are the worst," she told me. "Ill-tempered and lazy both."

"Lazy?" I asked. "Who's got time to be lazy?"

"Exactly," she answered. "And that's the whole trouble with you, Jericho Wetherby. You don't understand the merits of hard work. If it was up to you, you and that collie dog would be off chasing rabbits or otherwise stirring up mischief."

Now that was a fine idea! I would've accepted three good lickings just then to be off with Sandy and free of Jane Mary's complaining.

It got worse, though. We hadn't any of us had a thorough scrubbing since Sparta, and Jane Mary drew Ma's attention to the accumulation of mud on our hides.

"Well, it wouldn't hurt anybody to have a bath," Ma declared. So in addition to all our other chores, we wound up chopping extra wood and dragging pails of water from a spring Tuesday so Ma could ready her wooden tub, and we could all have a proper warm-water washing.

I believe there's a considerable distinction between how boys and girls view cleanliness. To Jane Mary, dirt was akin to plague, and she'd wash every chance. If there were females about to impress, Jake would dip himself in the river, but otherwise he was content to crust over like the rest of us.

"You boys smell like dogs," Jane Mary would complain.

"But we're partial to dogs," I'd answer, giving Sandy a pat on his head.

Ma generally didn't trouble us over bathing regularly, especially on the trail. So long as we appeared halfway human when visiting a town, she was satisfied. I guess Ma knew how hard it was to trudge through mud and dust and stay the same shade. But she took criticism to heart, so she ordered the bath.

Pa and Eli welcomed a hot-water soak, even if it did mean extra work stoking up a fire and boiling water. Jake deemed it tolerable, but he did regret we hadn't done it the day before when we had all that extra poplar wood handy. Me, all I could think of was how when my turn came around, the sun would be down, and I'd start freezing the moment I stepped out of the water.

That's just how it turned out, too. Even though Jake had a blanket ready and waiting, it took him and Eli rubbing hard to get the moisture out of my hide before I took a fever.

"Ma, the little ones could wait for morning," Jake suggested afterward.

"It would be warmer," I said through chattering teeth.

"There's never time to waste come sunrise," Pa objected. So Jordy and Josh had their baths that night, too.

I believe Jordy could have taken a bath at the North Pole and laughed about it after. He felt the cold, but it didn't trouble him like others. Josh, though, was a different story. He'd always been a trifle frail, and he came out of that bath a ball of goose bumps and shivers.

I was pretty well dry by then, and I helped Jake rub the chills out of Josh. He was just eight, and little for his age. It pure tore at your heart to see him shaking like that.

Jake and I each gave up a blanket that night so Josh could have extra, and we squeezed him between us, too. Even so, the night turned chill, and I woke up an hour after midnight to find Josh trembling with cold and wracked with fever.

"Jake," I whispered, shaking him awake. "Best fetch Ma."

Jake blinked his eyes awake, touched Josh's forehead, and hurried off. Wasn't any time at all before Pa rushed over, drew Josh up in his strong arms, and hurried to the wagon.

Since Jeremiah died, we'd all of us worried about Josh. I sat by the wagon the rest of the night, huddling with Jake, listening to Josh coughing and crying. Jane Mary and Ma rubbed his chest with alcohol and tried every tonic they knew. Pa even dosed Josh with cordial, which quieted the cough for a time. But come morning the fever raged, and Josh was beset by pain and spasms.

"You were right about the bath, Jacob," Ma lamented. "Why didn't I listen? I've lost three babies. Am I to lose another?"

Jane Mary was quiet for once. She walked off by herself and sat there waiting for the sun to come up.

"I didn't know," she told me when I passed her later, bound for the river with the water buckets.

I was halfway mad at her, and the temptation to heap on the blame was considerable. Just the same she was frantic with worry, and mean or not, she didn't need me adding to her pain.

"Nobody's blaming you," I finally said. "Everybody knows Josh's prone to fevers."

Jane Mary looked almost surprised. Without saying a word she pried a bucket from my hand and helped fetch the water. We didn't either of us speak, but I took her helping as a penance of sorts.

Josh wasn't any better by breakfast, and Ma was growing more worried by the minute. Pa occupied himself with chores, and he insisted we do likewise.

"Won't any of us get Josh better by setting off late," Pa argued. "Might be a doctor up the trail."

"Know what he sounds like?" Eli asked then. "My horse. Boys can come by a touch of colic, can't they? Have you tried the spirits of turpentine?"

"That's a horse cure!" Ma exclaimed.

"It is," Pa agreed, "but it's worth a try. Nothing else seems much use."

So Pa found his bottle of spirits of turpentine and tried that on Josh. Lo and behold wasn't long thereafter the coughing stopped, and Josh sank into a deep sleep. The fever broke around noon, and he was sitting up by late afternoon, chewing a square of cornbread and forcing a grin onto his face.

"Those spirits of turpentine'll cure anything," Eli said, shaking his head. "Might even try 'em on rickety bridges and rutted roads."

Past Campbellsville the country wasn't any too gentle, and I worried the rough road would plague Josh. He managed to sleep in spite of everything, though, snuggled in a dozen blankets, with Jane Mary or Ma tending his every need.

"Might be worth taking fever to get such treatment," Eli declared as he rode past Jordy and me.

"Not to me," Jordy whispered. "I can't abide Jane Mary poking and fawning on me. Rather have the pox."

We came by a fine, clear spring that afternoon, and we paused to eat and enjoy the fresh water. We also crossed the Natchez Trace, a good road that ran from the town of Natchez on the Mississippi north to Nashville. Was a world of travelers on the trace, and we halted long enough to watch some of them. Then it was on to Waynesboro, where we paid the steepest toll so far. Pa was able to change out some of his bank notes there, though, and we found prices fair at the Waynesboro shops.

"Might be prudent to put by supplies here," Eli suggested, and Pa agreed.

While Pa made the rounds of the Waynesboro shops and Ma dosed Josh again, Jake led Jordy and me off on an adventure.

"It's too early for hunting coons," I said as we started into the thick underbrush outside of town.

"And you didn't bring your rifle," Jordy added.

"Little brothers, I'm taking you exploring," Jake told us. "This'll be a real expedition, just like Lewis and Clark charting the Louisiana Territory for President Jefferson."

"How so?" I asked.

"Just look there and see for yourself," Jake advised. His finger pointed through the trees at a rocky ridge. There was a shadow just ahead, and once I studied it, I saw it was the entrance to a cave.

"I'm not fond of dark places," Jordy said, edging his way closer to me. "Wolves and bears and such take to caves in the winter, you know."

"That's why I invited Jer along," Jake answered. "He's fond of fighting bears, you know."

"I ought to bring Sandy then," I suggested. "Ma's got him tied back of the wagon, and he'd sure enjoy an adventure."

"No time," Jake insisted. "Come on!"

I started to argue, but Jake yanked us forward, and before I could object, we were all three of us stumbling inside that cave.

At first it wasn't much. Enough light filtered through the mouth of the cave to let us see. Later, though, as it opened up into a high cavern, I got uneasy. You couldn't see anything very clearly, and every step we took sent echoes booming through the place.

"This is really something, isn't it?" Jake asked as he lit a candle that he had brought and held it up. The light reflected off the sparkling limestone, giving the cave an eerie look to match its strange sounds and spooky feel. I halfway expected a haunt to walk right over and shake hands with us!

"Let's look around some more," Jake urged. Jordy and I shook our heads, but when Jake started off with the candle, we followed him. There were all sorts of narrow passages, some of them so small we had to crawl to get through.

"You're going to get us lost in here," I warned Jake.

"No," he argued. "I'm dropping wax from my candle along the way so we can retrace our steps."

"You can see wax in this place?" Jordy asked.

"So long as a bear's not after me," Jake replied.

Now that notion made us feel a whole lot safer!

"Jake, we best not hold Pa up," I said after we'd crawled down one passage and on to another.

"Ah, he'll be an hour packing the wagon," Jake grumbled. "But I guess you wouldn't have any use for treasure."

"Treasure?" Jordy asked.

"I heard about this cave from the livery boy," Jake explained. "Were some river pirates used the place for their hideout. Robbed folks along Duck River, or rode up to the Natchez Trace and preyed on travelers. Before they got caught they stole a thousand dollars in gold off a Nashville cotton buyer. That set the law on the pirates, and they were all caught save one. Story is that one holed up in this cave and starved. He had all the money with him. Fifty twenty-dollar gold pieces!"

"It's just a tale," I said, groaning. "Jake, somebody would've found any money stashed away here."

"Maybe," he admitted. "But maybe not."

He went on telling about the river pirate, who folks called One-Armed Ollie since he'd lost an arm to a musket ball. He was a fearsome fellow, all right. Jake said he used to murder children and eat their hearts. He drank blood, too. Jordy and I were getting downright nervous when Jake added how more than one town boy had come into this cave and never come out.

"Ole One-Armed Ollie must've been hungry," I suggested. I tried to laugh about it, but the place was full of strange sounds. Caves as a rule are dark and damp, too.

"Could be," Jake admitted. "We'll just look around a little more and head on back to Waynesboro."

"Fine by me," Jordy whispered. "In fact, we could go back right now."

Wasn't minutes later we all wished we'd followed Jordy's suggestion. I spied something shiny on the far wall, and Jake held his candle to it.

"Is it a coin?" I asked when Jake took the gold-looking object in his hand.

"Belt buckle," he said, disappointed.

"Look there to your left," Jordy cried.

Jake moved the candle over, and we howled. There at our feet was a pile of human bones. Without lingering,

I judged them to explain what had happened to those town boys. By the shape and size, they weren't big people, and the bones appeared to've been gnawed on.

"Jake!" I screamed.

"Come on," he urged.

We raced away, but the tunnel came to a dead end, and we frantically searched for the candle drippings.

"What's that sound?" Jordy whimpered.

I turned and stared at what seemed to be a haunt coming up the passage. Then, turning, I saw something even scarier behind Jake. It was a human skeleton, man-sized, but missing one arm.

"It's Ollie," I muttered, turning Jake around. "And that there's his haunt coming to get us."

We screamed, and the sound built into a series of echoes that close to deafened us. Jake held us still, though, insisting he'd find the treasure even if we had to be scared half to death. He did come across some rags, a knife, and a small hatchet. But as to Ollie's gold, if it had ever existed, it was hidden good.

Looking back down the passage, I could make out three shadows now, so I figured the haunts of those two eaten-up boys had joined Ollie. Any minute they'd fall on us. I grabbed Jordy's hand, elbowed Jake, and started down that passage. The shadows got bigger and bigger as we came nearer, and we were all hollering like lunatics now. But I figured to be a hard fellow to catch, running fast like I was, and I managed to escape the haunts. Jake and Jordy were close behind, and even though we had to crawl a hundred yards or so before popping out into the big cavern room, we eluded the haunts.

"Whew," I said, wiping sweat from my forehead. "That was sure close."

"Sure was," Jordy agreed.

"Oh, no," Jake muttered, lifting the candle higher. Behind us the three haunts rose like monstrous shadows. We yelled and scrambled away.

"Where's the wax?" Jake cried frantically. "Where?"

"There!" I yelled, leading the way toward a pair of wax dots. We glanced behind us, and the haunts were even bigger.

"One of 'em's got me!" Jordy screamed. A hand reached out and grabbed my leg then, and I fell to the slimy floor of the cave, shuddering with fear.

"You grabbed each other," Jake complained as he held the candle over us. "Look. The shadows are gone."

"No, they're there," I said, pointing to the other wall.

"Oh, no," Jake said, dropping to his knees and laughing like a loon.

"What's wrong?" I asked.

"The haunts," he said, drawing us to him. "The candle. Look!"

Jordy figured it out before me. He shook his head and covered his face. Then I caught on. Those haunts were our own fool shadows. In that dark place, our candlelight cast them on the walls.

"We could've stayed and searched out the treasure," Jake grumbled. "Come on. There's still time."

"Maybe it was a shadow," I said. "And maybe it was a haunt. You didn't see any gold before. But we saw those bones plain enough."

"Sure did," Jordy agreed.

"Me," I added, "that's all I need to remember. I had enough adventuring, Jake. You want that treasure, go back and get it your own self."

"Yeah," Jordy said, standing. "Jer and I are getting out of this place right now."

"You can't be afraid of shadows?" Jake cried.

"No, but where there's bones, there's haunts," I declared. "Everybody knows that. Leave 'em to guard their treasure, Jake. Can't have been much fun dying in that dark place and getting eaten by a cannibal pirate."

"Well, somebody probably did find the treasure," Jake admitted as he followed us outside. "It was a mighty fine adventure, though."

Jordy and I stared at him in amazement. Jake's notion of a high time and mine were considerably different.

CHAPTER EIGHT

THAT SKELETON CAVE PUT AN END TO OUR ADVENTURING for a while. Pa was put out with us over straying, and I don't think Jordy or I either one slept too sound that night. Every hoot owl and mourning dove in the river bottoms brought shivers down my backbone, and I half-way believed ole One-Armed Ollie would pay a visit to our camp!

"We should have had another look for that treasure," Jake complained as we gathered firewood the next morning.

"We've got enough worries without bringing down haunts on us," I told him.

Actually, though, we got along just fine the rest of that week. Josh shed his cough, and by Friday he was back walking the trail with Jordy and me. We made close to twenty miles each day, and Friday afternoon Jake and I snagged seven fat catfish out of the Tennessee River near Savannah. We had a real fine fish fry afterward. Pa complained of spending two dollars on the ferry that got us across the Tennessee, but he was ready enough to pay a whiskey peddler forty cents for a jug.

"Used all the cordial on Josh," he explained as he took a pull on the jug. "Can't be without medicines, you know."

"Just bought it for a cure, huh?" Jake asked as Pa sipped a bit more. "You ailing, Pa?"

"Had to taste it to make sure it hadn't gone sour," he explained. "There's no need worrying your ma about it, either."

Jake nudged me, and we grinned. Ma was dead set against strong spirits. Wasn't likely she'd tolerate that jug.

West of Savannah, we found ourselves in cotton country. You knew it from the higher price of corn and fodder if not from the wagons hauling cotton bales to Memphis. The road was crowded with them and folks headed to Texas. I thought we traveled heavy till I spied one batch of Nashville families hauling stoves, furniture, and big trunks tied one atop another.

"Poor horses won't make Arkansas," Eli observed.

I agreed. Some of those wagons were straining a team of oxen!

Sandy had a real time of it. Were dogs to chase and

sheep to nip. From time to time we'd share a camp with other Texas-bound folks, and when the sun was warm enough, Jake and I would swim off the wearies in a creek or pond and swap tales with some of the other boys. I'd make a friend or two, but in no time we'd pull ahead, and they'd just wave at us from the trail.

"Be glad when we settle someplace," Jordy muttered. "I've near worn down my shoes to nothing, and I'm pure tired of salt pork and cornbread."

"Come November you'll remember this stretch as heaven," Eli warned. "Worse country's up ahead."

Sure didn't seem so, though. Once we crossed Hatchie River on the ferry, we rolled all the way to Bolivar. We weren't more than half a week shy of Memphis now, and the tales of folks passing eastward gave us high expectations of the mighty Mississippi and the fine town built on the Chickasaw Bluffs there.

It being the Sabbath when we passed through Bolivar, Ma got us scrubbed some and led us into the church there for some sermonizing. Sitting in that stuffy hall with the town folk giving us a wary eye, I almost wished Ma had insisted on a dip in the river. We smelled of wet leather, catfish, and axle grease, and the preacher hurried himself through his words on our account.

"I'm delighted you were able to share our service," he told Ma afterward.

"I apologize for our state," she replied. "My youngest

caught a cough at his last bath, and I fret of the harm another might bring."

"Rightly so," the preacher said, nodding somberly. "We have a lot of travelers passing through, and it's not their garments the Lord sees."

I don't think too many folks agreed with him, though. A gang of boys pelted us with pebbles and urged on our departure.

"We couldn't stay anyway," Pa announced.

Ma was sour the rest of the day, though.

"We'll avoid towns if we can't be presentable," she vowed.

That night we came across a family called Clarke, camped on a hill outside town. They looked bone weary and trail sore, and we were amazed to learn they'd come out from Carolina.

"You got yourself a good camp made," I told the Clarkes' boy, Andy.

"Always do on Sunday," he told me. "We don't travel, you see. Ma won't allow it."

"My ma's not much in favor of it, either," I told him. "Only Pa insists."

"Well, your ma's not quite so big as mine," Andy pointed out. I admit he had a point. Mrs. Clarke was a fair-sized woman, and though she seemed agreeable enough, Andy warned it wasn't wise to get her riled.

Mr. Clarke wasn't any too small, either, but Andy wasn't so much as a sneeze bigger than me, and we were both twelve.

"Ma says I take after my uncles," Andy explained.

"That's what my family says of me," I said, grinning. We were both of us friends thereafter.

Toward dusk we had other company. The Packards came from the west, and to look at them, Eli'd been easy on the country. Mr. and Mrs. Packard were sad-eyed and terrible thin. Their two girls were wearing dresses made of burlap. The boys, and there were four of them, were fearful puny things. Even the oldest, who I judged about ten, had trouble keeping his overall straps on his bony shoulders.

"You look to've had a hard time of it," Mrs. Clarke said when she brought the Packards a bushel of potatoes.

"It's Texas," Mrs. Packard declared. "The fires of perdition scorch the place in summer, and the winter chills'll freeze your bones! Mosquitoes, snakes, scorpions, coyotes, Indians . . ."

"Texas has got everything in it that can kill a man," Mr. Packard added. "And not a one of 'em pleasant."

"Nonsense," Eli argued. "There's wonderful pasture for grazing, good farmland along the rivers, and—"

"Mister, I been there three years and never seen any of that," Mr. Packard said, spitting. "Look at my boys! They're stunted sure. I buried two babies in that god-forsaken place, and I won't plant another. No, sir, we're going back to the Cumberland country where a man can get an honest return on his labors."

"Amen!" Mrs. Packard shouted.

A bit later she stepped over to our fire and smiled a snaggle-toothed grin. "Tell me, do you suppose I could beg some milk off your cow?" she asked.

"Jake, see if Cathy's got something to spare," Pa instructed.

"Is Texas really so bad?" Jordy asked her.

"Worse'n any nightmare I ever had," Mrs. Packard answered. Her eyes sort of lost their spark, and she stared at her toes. "Never once got a decent crop in before drought or hail or grass fires hit. Nobody to talk to for miles. And if you don't watch out, some band of savage Indians'll come along and snatch your youngsters!"

"Eli?" Ma asked, turning to him. "How certain are you of your information? I know my brother Daniel, and he's prone to exaggerate."

Eli waited for Jake to finish the milking before responding.

"Thanks kindly," Mrs. Packard said when she accepted the half-full bucket. "And if you've any sense, you'll turn back while there's time."

Once Mrs. Packard was out of hearing, Eli rose and studied the fire. "Ma'am," he said, turning to Ma, "it's no harder to make a go of it in Texas than in Tennessee. Some don't manage it anywhere. Weak people don't survive, but I don't number us among them. It's a country of high hopes, and your young ones can find a happy future there. I'm going myself, aren't I?"

"But that woman," Ma said, shuddering. "She looked to have been through a world of pain."

"Didn't put her above begging milk," Eli noted. "And she's over at the Clarke camp now, askin' other favors, I suspect."

"Wouldn't you if your family was starving?" Ma asked.

"I'd send my boys to the river to fish some," Eli replied. "And I'd have my husband take his rifle and look for a squirrel to shoot."

"He's right," Pa agreed. "Folks can't expect somebody to just hand them their supper. There's effort involved."

Even so the hollow look of the Packards and their mournful singing later on had us wondering some.

Except for a couple of hard rains, the weather was almost pleasant. The Clarkes trailed along behind us, so Andy walked at my elbow, spattering mud on me and telling spook stories. Once Jordy and I shared our cave tale, he turned to other subjects, though. As for the country, it was miles and miles of Negroes picking cotton. Twice we were held up by lines of wagons hauling the crop to gins or else transporting bales to Memphis. One time I counted over three hundred in one line!

The fine houses there, surrounded by all sorts of little buildings, put Knoxville's best to shame. Jordy counted twenty windows in the front of one of those houses. White-painted rail fences bounded horse pastures full of sleek thoroughbreds. Wednesday night we camped on a sliver of creek beside the road. It promised to be good coon-hunting land, but a carriage rolled up with a couple of dandified young fellows in it to announce we were squatting on the Havelock plantation.

"Y'all are welcome to stay the night and water your animals," the older of the young men announced, "but you must depart tomorrow. Understand?"

"We hear quite well," Eli replied, making a mocking bow. "I thank you for the hospitality. As for leaving, we generally ride with the sun."

"That would be best," the second one said. "All sorts are drawn to Shelby County, and we prefer most to hurry along to Arkansas."

"Do our best to see you're not troubled with us more than's necessary," Pa promised. Once they'd left, Pa and Eli dug out the Savannah jug and had a sip or two. Ma and Jane Mary were up the creek, washing themselves and their clothes. Once they returned, Jake had us in the freezing stream, scraping mud and such off our hides.

"You people wash too much," Andy complained as he watched from the bank. "I don't mind an idle Sunday or even a bit of versifying, but I'd never stomach regular baths."

Didn't take us a minute to rush up and drag him in with us. It was cold as ice, that creek, but with all the splashing and foolishness that followed, I don't think we any of us minded so much. Sandy even jumped in for a time.

We rolled into Memphis on Thursday, the twenty-eighth day of October. It was about the biggest town I'd ever seen, and by far the finest.

"Like a scene out of *Vanity Fair*," Ma remarked. I knew what she meant. There was a picture in one of Grandma's books of a town full of fine people and neat houses. That was Memphis, all right!

While Pa changed out the rest of his Tennessee bank notes, we boys hurried down to the riverbanks. The Mississippi appeared to be a mile wide there, and we stared in amazement at the small boats and barges passing along below the bluff. Huge steamboats went by now and then, churning up the river with their sidewheels as they made their way down to New Orleans or up to St. Louis. The banks were covered with cotton bales, and the surface of the river was painted white with loose lint.

"You boys don't mean to pass the day staring at the wharves, do you?" Eli called.

"Not much else to do," Jake replied.

"Nonsense," Eli argued. "Your pa's sent me to find you. He's got a silver dollar for each of you. Spend it as you may."

"Now that's a real treasure!" Jordy exclaimed, hurrying away. Josh and Jake followed. I read Andy's disappointment and nudged his ribs.

"Bet I can find some stick candy," I whispered. "Enough for two."

"Figure so?" he asked, grinning.

"Don't see why not," I said, matching his smile. "You had a bath, didn't you? Won't anybody complain about us visiting their store."

"Stick candy's close to be worth a bath," he admitted, waving me toward Eli. "Almost."

When we met Pa outside the bank, he passed over the promised dollars, and we soon found ourselves surrounded by merchants and peddlers hawking bread, fruit, toys, and even silver jewelry. I satisfied myself with stick candy and a pocketknife. Josh bought himself a whole basket of cherries! Jordy picked up some sugar taffy, and Jake came by a buckskin vest. Jane Mary wasted her dollar on a book of maps. I figured that a waste since she was smart enough already!

Pa handed over seven dollars to a fellow for a quality coat.

"I have to make a proper impression on those Texans," he explained.

He also bought flour, bacon, sugar, coffee, and molasses—twenty whole dollars' worth. For another ten he purchased a five-shot Colt percussion revolver.

"You'll need that in Texas," Eli had said, and Pa trusted him to know.

Once everything was paid for, we loaded up the wagon and headed down to the steamboat landing. The Clarkes were waiting for us there, grim-faced and solemn.

"It's no bargain getting across," Mr. Clarke announced. "And no fording the Father of Waters."

"How much?" Pa asked.

"Four dollars for us," Mr. Clarke said. "Five and six bits for your outfit and the family. Some swim, but it's dangerous."

"Pay the money, Joe," Ma insisted. "Too many Wetherby boys have already drowned in rivers."

Pa nodded sadly and counted out the money. A short time later a man helped Pa get the wagon aboard the steamboat. We followed along on foot. It wasn't until the boat got out into the river that we saw just how pretty Memphis really appeared and sensed the power of the Mississippi.

"It'd take a mighty strong man to swim that stream," Andy told me. "Thought to try her, only I knew you'd want to come, too."

"Oh?" I asked, sensing a jab coming.

"And before we got halfway over, we'd be wrestling each other. Drown for sure."

I grinned, and he bit off a chunk of stick candy. Crossing the Mississippi you almost got to feeling dandy.

CHAPTER NINE

Arkansas was different from the first. Mostly we found ourselves crossing wet bottoms on narrow lanes that sometimes entirely disappeared in small ponds. To call the trail a road was a stretch of the imagination. And yet it seemed somebody was collecting a toll for passage every few miles.

Pa dubbed the toll collectors and their gates "Arkansas shaving machines."

"They shave our money down a sliver at a time," he declared. "And they claim this swamp trail's a road! I've seen a boar make a better trail without half trying!"

By Friday we'd cleared the worst of the Mississippi bottoms. But a wind howled up, and rain lashed us so that we had to turn the wagon sideways and huddle together to keep from being blown back to Memphis. The Clarkes near tipped over, but Eli and Pa managed to throw ropes over the wheels and right them. Afterward Andy splashed over and hunkered down between Jordy and me.

"This's worse'n a creek bath," he grumbled.

"How'd you know?" Jordy asked. "You never take baths."

"Why, I took one with you fellows back in Tennessee," Andy argued. "Wasn't by choice, I'll grant you, but it did educate me some on Wetherby habits."

"A man could benefit from such examples," I said, laughing in spite of the rain.

We were wet as sponges by the time the rain let up. It wasn't being soggy that troubled Pa, though. It was the lake that surrounded us.

"How does a body find the trail when it's flooded?" Pa asked Eli.

"Somebody rides ahead and marks it," Eli explained.

Even so we got stuck more than once. We weren't the only ones, though. Approaching Fish Lake a party of Georgians was bogged down proper. Wasn't a wagon didn't have itself sunk to the axles in mud, and their tired horses were overmatched.

"Job thought *he* had troubles!" the Georgians' redheaded leader, Mr. Hawkins, complained.

"We might be able to help out," Pa said, waving me over. "Jericho, don't you figure a fellow with hair red as yours deserves a favor?"

I looked over at Mr. Hawkins, and he laughed.

"Sure do, Pa," I agreed. "Want to give the Morgans a try at those wagons?"

"Unhitch 'em," Pa said, and I started in on the harness. Jake climbed down from his horse and lent a hand, and we soon had our four animals pulling with the Georgia horses. One by one the Georgians rolled out of their trap.

"I'd pay you something for your trouble," Mr. Hawkins said when Jake and I took charge of the Morgans.

"Pa?" I called.

"Couldn't take money for doing a fellow traveler such a little help," Pa said, refusing the money.

"Not to mention a redhead," I added.

"Well, you'll share our camp and let us cook you up some Georgia sausages," Mr. Hawkins declared. "Give your women a rest one night."

"Fair enough," Pa agreed.

So after crossing Fish Lake on a raft ferry, we passed the evening chewing spicy sausage and baked beans with the Georgians. They were headed for Texas, too, but were losing heart.

"We've had sickness aplenty, and of late we've met a fair number of wagons headed east out of Texas, sharing fearful tales."

"We've heard some of those ourselves," Pa confessed. "But my brother-in-law's found us a parcel of land to settle, and it's a fine chance for the youngsters."

"There's always some who fail to meet the mark," Eli added. "Me, I plan to test myself."

That next day the swamps got worse, though, and the rain returned. We'd never really dried ourselves from Friday, and I was beginning to lose feeling in my toes. Jake could wring water out of his shirt and laugh about it. I just trudged along, grumbling and wondering why we'd left home in the first place.

Actually we fared better than most. Some of the people we passed had weak horses, and many tried to tote too much. We passed wagons with broken axles that had left travelers afoot. Others smashed wheels or went off the trail into a hollow. Bogs held everybody up now and then, and it was a sight to see dainty ladies in fine dresses pushing wagons through knee-deep mud.

"Looks like the mud people have returned," Jake pointed out when we passed a whole family of Georgians coated with goo.

"We're not much better ourselves," Jordy said, laughing. "And sure to get worse."

Wasn't an hour afterward that the trail turned into a swamp, and we got ourselves properly stuck. Even the Morgans couldn't budge the wagon, and we had to unload every trunk and barrel. Even so, with the Morgans hauling and us Wetherbys pushing, the wagon only slid sideways a hair.

"Looks like you've found trouble this time," a familiar voice called then. I turned around and saw Mr.

Hawkins gazing down from his wagon. "Could you use a fellow redhead's help, Jericho?" he asked.

"Could sure use somebody's," I answered.

The whole of the Georgia company piled out and helped us push our wagon. When that didn't free the wheels, they brought over their best horses, and with extra effort, our wagon finally sloshed its way out of that swamp.

"Looks like it's my turn to offer thanks," Pa said, shaking Mr. Hawkins's hand.

"Well, a favor's never wasted on a Georgian," Mr. Hawkins replied. "He's sure to pay it back if given a chance."

Pa pulled up short that day, and the Georgians passed us by. Mr. Hawkins rubbed his hair and waved when he rolled along. I do believe that's the first time I ever deemed red hair a value. We made camp atop a knoll, us on one side of a spring and the Clarke wagon on the other. I wished we'd had the chance to offer the Georgians some Tennessee ham, but they were bound on making miles, so we settled for Carolina company.

Sandy scared up some rabbits that night, as it turned out, and Jake shot two. We turned them on a spit, and it proved a welcome relief from salt pork and cornbread. The sky cleared, and Eli had us boys staring at stars and figuring their shapes. Orion the Hunter was easy enough, what with his belt of stars, but some of the others were a real puzzlement. Andy picked 'em up fast, though, and afterward he told me he had an uncle who'd been a sailor for a time.

"I feel like one myself hereabouts," Andy added. "Most days I'm swimming more'n walking."

Next morning was Sunday, the final day of October. Ma had us up early, listening to her read Scripture. We prayed for better weather, good health, and continued safety. After breakfast when Jake and I readied the Morgans, Mr. Clarke chatted with Pa. I realized we'd be parting company, what with Mrs. Clarke still refusing to stir on a Sunday, and Pa insisting we continue our journey.

"We'll see you on down the trail," Andy told me hopefully.

"Or maybe in Texas," I said, waving good-bye. Sandy danced over and gave Andy a face licking. Then Pa hollered it was time to get moving, and I hurried on my way.

We heard cheers up the trail for miles that morning, and I expected us to come upon a camp meeting. Turned out that wasn't the reason at all. We'd finally found dry ground, and we raised a yell or two ourselves. The roads could still be rutted and muddy, but at least we could see our toes again.

Was Monday, crossing the St. Francis River, that we had the strangest experience of our travels. There was a ferry there to take wagons across, and folks swam their animals and youngsters over at a ford downstream. An old trapper would take people across in his canoe for two bits, and he was doing a better business than the ferry.

"Too bad you can't haul wagons in them canoes," a Kentuckian lamented.

"Who says I can't?" the trapper cried. "Lash the fool boats together, and we can get you across."

"How much?" the Kentuckian asked.

"A dollar," the trapper answered. "Ferry wants three."

The wife of that Kentuckian argued against it, but the trapper had his bargain. In no time the trapper managed somehow to get the right-hand wagon wheels into one canoe and the left-hand wheels into the other. The wagon then started across.

I near fell over laughing at it. The ferryman was stomping on his hat and cursing considerably. Most folks pointed in amazement at the wagon floating across the St. Francis. The trapper paddled, and the wagon sailed on along. Then we noticed the canoes seemed to go down a hair in front. Then in back. Sure enough, halfway across the boats were taking on water.

"Paddle faster, Zeke!" the Kentuckian pleaded. "Faster!"

"Doin' my best, friend," the trapper answered. But a full thirty feet short of the far bank, water poured over the sides of those canoes, and the wagon sank like a stone to the bottom. Oh, a few wood barrels and furniture boards rose to the surface, but mostly those Kentuckians lost everything. The trapper was swimming for his life—not afraid of drowning but powerfully alarmed at the rifle the Kentuckian's wife was aiming in his direction.

"We're ruined," the Kentuckian said, sobbing as his wife did her best to punish that trapper.

"Well, it was a fine thing to see, wasn't it?" the ferryman asked. "Tell you what. I'll take you and your horses across free, and start your recovery off with five silver dollars."

Others pitched in, too, and the Kentuckians' loss was made a bit less painful. The ferryman upped his price, though, now the trapper was gone, so we didn't much benefit by the riverman's generosity.

From the St. Francis to Little Rock, we were shaved regular. Every river had a toll bridge or a ferry, and the farther west, the steeper the price. There were plenty of toll gates on the road, too, and it was common to pay two or three dollars at each. You could make a try at going around, but with swamps and bayous aplenty, few risked it. As to refusing payment, those Arkansas barbers kept shotgun-toting cousins handy in case of trouble.

November brought early sunsets and cold nights. We were managing twenty miles most every day, though, for the Morgans were used to the work, and we boys managed the walking better.

"Nothing at all to walking twenty miles these days," Jordy boasted.

"Not so long as it stays dry," I added.

"It won't," Josh said, sighing. Sandy barked his agreement, and I kicked a rock across the road.

We were camped on a ridge overlooking the west bank of the White River the fourth of November. The road on either side of the river had been muddy, and the ground, though high, was damp. There was plenty of timber, though, and Eli showed us how to weave sticks into a sort of thatched bed. That way we were up off the ground.

We made a shelter of sorts between two boulders, and it proved a blessing when the skies emptied around dusk, tormenting us with rain and hail.

"You had to talk about easy going, didn't you?" Josh complained, clamping an arm onto Jordy's head.

"That didn't cause the rain," Jordy insisted as he fought to free himself.

"Maybe it did," Jake said, prying the boys apart. "No help for it now. Thank Eli for our roof and get some rest. Road's sure to be wet tomorrow."

Truth is, it was wet thereafter, and it took a different sort of toll on us. We made poor progress, and we were prickly to a fault. Our clothes were generally soggy, and my toes finally broke through the thin leather of my shoes. Even at midday Josh shivered some, and when possible Jake would haul him on Red. Jordy and I splashed on by ourselves, and one of us was spattering the other with mud most of the day. It brought on elbowing and a set-to now and then.

"We're all of us worn down," Pa announced Saturday

night. "Little Rock's close by, and we wouldn't want to get there on a Sunday. We need supplies."

"Need a rest and a bath even more," Ma noted.

"Well, you don't favor Sunday traveling anyway, Mary Elizabeth," Pa observed. "We'll lay up a day, mend clothes, scrub children, and do some serious praying."

"Amen!" we shouted.

We truly did need the rest, for it showed up right away in our faces. Even Jane Mary seemed in a good humor. Though Jake and I near wore ourselves to a frazzle chopping wood to heat water, we all welcomed a warm soak. Stepping into dry clothes was even better. Then later, while Jordy and Josh dried their toes beside the fire, Jake motioned me toward the wagon.

"Never did get you a proper cap, Jer," he said. "Feel up to a little hunting?"

"Was born ready," I replied. "Can Sandy come?"

"That dog's likely to be more use than either of us. Fetch him."

So it was that the three of us started along the ridge in search of game. Jake shot a pair of squirrels out of an oak tree, and Sandy ran down a ten-pound cottontail. Then I spied a wisp of white to my left and nudged Jake.

"Deer," I whispered.

The mere hint of venison steaks widened Jake's eyes, and he followed my finger to where the deer was making its way through the thick brush. I expected him to take aim, but instead he passed the rifle to me.

"You found him," he explained. "You shoot him."

Now I was a fair murderer of pinecones and tree branches back home, but the biggest live thing I'd ever shot was a rabbit. Still, shooting was shooting. Or so I thought. That deer was close to invisible, blending its hide into the trees. It had a head full of antlers, seven points at least, but they were about all you could see in the fading light. There was the tail, but only a fool would shoot a deer in the rump!

I crept a little closer and rested the long rifle barrel on a handy hickory branch. Then I took aim. I was knotted up tense, but Jake gave me a tap on the shoulder and assured me I'd do fine. I took a deep breath, let it out, and squeezed the trigger. The rifle exploded, knocking me back a foot or so, and powder smoke stung my eyes. Sandy yelped in surprise, then raced off after the deer. It raced away, and I thought I'd missed. Three or four bounds were all it managed before falling, though.

"You shot him true, Jer!" Jake exclaimed. "Now all we got to do's find you a coon."

I didn't give a hoot about a skin cap just then. I'd sew myself some buckskin moccasins to replace my worn-out shoes, and we'd have antlers for buttons, fresh meat for our bellies, and bones for Sandy to chew.

CHAPTER TEN

AFTER SHOOTING THAT DEER, I CONSIDERED MYSELF A frontiersman of some repute. And in truth, we Wetherbys were trail-toughened veterans, having rolled through Tennessee and half of Arkansas in the month since leaving home. We passed through Little Rock November 9, and Eli told us it was all downhill to Texas now.

November brought a new cold to the nights, though, and Pa paid out some of his precious dollars for wool blankets at a Little Rock mercantile. Josh, in particular, slept better thereafter. At Rockport Pa bought ginger-bread from a lady, declaring children needed a taste of ginger now and then to put a shine in their eyes. I believe he was almost a child himself, gobbling that gingerbread. Later he confessed he'd thought to have lost a pouch of gold pieces back up the trail. Turned out he'd stuffed them in his trunk and forgot. Two hundred dollars found could cheer a man known to count pennies considerably.

Pa bought sweet potatoes and pork ribs at a Ouachita River trading post. I welcomed the sweet potatoes for their variety, but I would have preferred venison for meat.

"Game turns scarce up ahead, boys," Eli warned. "It's best to be certain."

We did have a fair portion of our deer smoked and waiting, but I enjoyed the hunt. I'd go whenever Eli and Jake set out, mainly on account of Sandy's talent for sniffing out game, and Jake would offer me his rifle from time to time. Wasn't long before I had my coonskin cap. Jordy and Josh had theirs a hair later.

The high country of central Arkansas had been a welcome relief from the muddy swamps along the Mississippi. Even when it rained, which was often, there were mounds of pine needles to make a dry nest to sleep on. We built shelters whenever there was enough light left when Pa located our camp, and the occasional farmer would offer us his porch or barn.

Just outside Antoine a family named Hollis put us up on their fine place, stuffed us with ham and sausage, and insisted on hearing of our adventures. Their youngsters were smallish, with the eldest, a little fellow named Tim, being Josh's age. Jake told 'em of our cave adventure, and I fear it was a poor return on their kindness. Those children were awake most of the night.

After leaving Antoine, we found ourselves in rough, thin-looking country. The cold tormented us, and Josh grew feverish. Wasn't long afterward Eli's horse took sick, too, and Eli himself went pale with fever the day we forded the Little Missouri.

"Winter's come," Pa said, frowning. "And we're still a long way from Texas."

With Eli riding in the wagon, Jordy and I took turns leading his horse. Sometimes I'd tie the bay behind the wagon, and we'd do some exploring. A lot of people had come through Arkansas lately, and some of their broken-down wagons stood beside the trail. Others had had to leave heavy trunks and all sorts of furniture behind. Once or twice we passed what looked to be a whole city without walls. Most of those goods had been gone through by road pirates or travelers, but you could come by something useful if you looked hard enough. Ma got some calico to patch Jane Mary's dresses one time, and we swapped an unbroken rib from a wagon's cover for one of ours that was splintered past saving.

I came by the real treasure in the Sabine bottoms—a fiddle of fine polished wood resting in its leather case. A note attached read, "Pray God a musical sort finds this fiddle. My boy Freddie's gone to glory and will play it no more."

I showed it to Ma, who deemed it a poor notion.

"That fiddle should go to someone with the skill to play it properly," she declared.

"Come first snow, it'll be ruined," Jake argued.

"I'd judge it to be worth money," Pa said, rubbing the wood and eyeing the strings. "Fine workmanship. We can always sell it, Mary Elizabeth."

"You remember that fellow back in Tennessee?" I said, snatching back the fiddle. "Didn't he say I was musical? Give me a chance, and I'll figure it out."

"Can't hurt, I suppose," Pa muttered.

The next day or so, I'm not sure Pa believed that. I made some mighty peculiar sounds. Jane Mary complained bitterly, and Sandy howled worse than a coyote. Then a farmer showed me how to tighten the strings. I managed considerable improvement afterward.

"It's a regular wonder," Jake remarked to me one day when we were building the supper cook fire. "You make a fair sound with that thing, little brother."

And I got better. The music brought on smiles, and we warmed ourselves that November singing to the fiddle.

I like to think the good time we made through Arkansas was partly due to my fiddling, but we were pretty well clear of the state when I produced my first passable tunes. No, it was winter that hurried us along in spite of the bad roads, costly ferries, infernal shaving machines, and sickness. When we crossed Red River, I knew we were closing in, and on November 18, camped beside a small spring overlooking a world of red soil and high, thick cane, Eli announced we were in Texas at last.

"Not much of a border to cross, is there?" Jordy asked.

"It's not the Mississippi," Eli admitted. "But there's a smell to the air. Opportunity!"

"Is that it?" Jane Mary grumbled. "I just figured the boys needed a wash!"

She couldn't dampen our spirits, though. That night Ma baked the last of our Arkansas sweet potatoes, which we had with a fat hen and boiled collard greens. Afterward we sang and danced and recorded the event in the family Bible.

"Wetherbys in Texas, 18 November, 1852."

The next morning, a Friday, we were greeted by a chill fog. Ice painted everything in sight, including our eyebrows and blankets.

"Lord," Jordy said, shivering. "The mud people've been frozen!"

Needless to say, we got into our overalls in record time. Jake and I lit a fire, and everyone huddled around it, warming their hands and coughing the ice from their lungs.

"How much farther now, Eli?" Ma asked.

"Few days," he told us. "Unless the road freezes."

"Don't know about the road," Jordy whispered, "but I'm froze now."

So were considerable patches of the road, and we only managed ten miles that day. There were farms thereabouts to sell us fodder for our horses and poor old Cathy, and the woods were heavy with post and blackjack oaks, so we had plenty of good firewood for our camp.

"Tomorrow we'd best do better," Eli warned, though. "Look at those clouds. I'll wager they're carrying snow!"

"Didn't know it snowed in Texas," Jake said. "Everybody's always talking about the heat."

"That's summer," Eli explained. "Winter can be as rough. Even worse on travelers."

I judged it so, for Saturday I was pure numb with the cold. It started raining early on, and the road was soon more river than wagon trail.

"I'm freezing!" Josh cried around midday, and Eli pulled him up on the bay. Jordy rode behind Jake a bit later. Sandy and I sloshed along by ourselves, trying to ignore the numbing cold and darkening skies.

We got into Clarksville, the first genuine Texas town of the trip, and Pa spent eleven dollars on supplies. We ate well enough, but the rain never let up. Even camped beneath the wagon, resting on a mountain of oak leaves, we couldn't get dry. Josh wound up in the wagon with Ma, Pa, and Jane Mary. Eli, Jake, Jordy, and I squeezed together, shivering with cold, and prayed the sun would break through next morning.

It didn't. Instead the skies choked with snowflakes, and a world of white fluff descended on us. I woke up to find a foot of snow blanketing the land. The horses were stomping restlessly, and poor Cathy had broken loose.

"Sandy?" I called, noticing him gone from my side.

Sandy yelped his answer from a prickly thicket. He and Cathy had found refuge in a cedar grove.

"Jake, Eli, Jordy," I called, shaking them awake. "It's snowing!"

"Sure," Jake moaned, pulling his blankets closer.

"Get up!" I urged.

"I can't," Jordy whimpered. "My feet are froze together."

I laughed, but he wasn't joking. The water had saturated his blankets, and they'd frozen solid. His feet might as well have been in leg irons! I had to cut him free with a knife.

Jake and Eli shook themselves awake after I pried Jordy out of his bed. The four of us collected the Morgans, the saddle horses, and Cathy. To our horror, we discovered our last four chickens and ole Hannibal, the rooster, were frozen dead in their coop. The wagon wheels were trapped, and icicles dangled from the cover.

"You think that odd?" Jake whispered. "You got icicles in your hair, Jer."

I did, too. Near every inch of me was frozen, so it wasn't so surprising. Even so, Pa deemed us in serious trouble.

"What do we do?" he asked, staring at the wintry landscape surrounding us.

"Well, we can't stay here," Jake declared. "Not even Ma'd have us do that, and it's Sunday."

"No choice," Eli declared. "There's nothing ahead for miles. Turn back to Clarksville and see if we can find shelter."

That's what we did. It grated on us retracing our steps, but the snow was getting thicker, and it was all Jordy and I could do to stumble ahead in the snow. Josh was snuggled between Ma and Jane Mary, but he was coughing hard just the same. Our faces were red, and our fingers were growing blue. I couldn't feel my toes, and my teeth rattled with every wind gust.

"There's light just ahead," Pa called. "Eli, best we ride ahead and find help."

"Yes, sir," Eli answered, and the two of them struggled up the snowbound trail. Jake remained.

"Somebody's got to see you there, little brothers," he told us. But though he tried to make a joke of the snow and the cold, his eyes betrayed his fear.

We were still a hundred yards or so shy of Clarksville when a small army of bundled folk descended on us. A burly man climbed atop the wagon and took charge. Two others threw a heavy blanket around my shoulders and dragged me along toward town. I halfway fainted, but it didn't matter. That fellow had me, and he got me to a small frame building and on out of the wet and cold.

"What's this place?" I asked.

"Schoolhouse," he answered. "Don't have much use

of it on Sundays. Now hush up and shed those clothes. I got my boy coming along with dry things. First get over to that stove and warm yourself."

Now normally I'm shy with strangers, but the cold'll plumb take charge of your mind and leave you addled. I got a couple of buttons open, but my fingers were frozen. Before I knew it, that fellow was stripping off my clothes like you'd skin a rabbit. Me, twelve whole years old, standing bare-hide naked beside the stove, dripping while a boy rubbed me dry with a saddle blanket.

I would've been shamed by the whole business if Jake and Jordy weren't at my elbows, letting those Clarksville folks do the same thing to them. Turned out Eli and Pa were over next door at the mercantile, getting like treatment. Ma, Jane Mary, and Josh, being less soaked, were helped along to the parson's house and got easier treatment.

"Can't complain much," Jake told me when we huddled in our blankets beside the stove. "Another hour and we'd have been frozen worse'n Hannibal!"

Those Clarksville folks took us right into their hearts. They offered us such clothes and blankets as they could spare, and we had the use of the schoolhouse the whole day. A liveryman tended our horses and gave Cathy a stall in his barn. The parson put up Ma and Jane Mary, and his boy put Sandy in a neighbor's barn. We men, meanwhile, strung lines and hung up clothing all over the school. Wasn't a stitch we owned hadn't gotten wet, and most things were frozen.

Around noon the sky lightened some, and the snow stopped. The parson, a Kentucky fellow named Nalley, offered us some comforting words, and his wife brought over a basket of food.

"How can we repay such kindness?" Pa asked, pulling out his coin purse.

"The Lord expects the faithful to aid pilgrims," Parson Nalley answered. "We welcome the chance to help."

After we'd thawed out and dried up, Pa gathered the family together. We gave thanks for our deliverance, and Monday Pa spent what he could afford in Clarksville.

"This is a fine town, with good people," Ma observed. "Not a bad place to settle, wouldn't you say so, Joe?"

"I would," Pa agreed. "But Dan's bought land elsewhere. Best we enjoy this break in the weather and continue our journey."

So Monday we said our good-byes, thanked everyone, and set out across the snow-covered land headed west.

CHAPTER ELEVEN

BY TUESDAY THE WEATHER HAD FAIRED UP SOME. WE welcomed the sun's brief return, but by noon, when we rolled into Paris, the seat of Lamar County, it had clouded over again.

"Don't take such gloomy skies to heart," Eli advised when we loaded a bushel of meal into the wagon and prepared to resume our journey. "Texas weather favors change, and it may go and get better by nightfall."

It didn't, but we refused to let that bother us.

"Best thing to do's stay busy," Jake suggested, so we went hunting. There being few trees thereabouts, we had little luck locating deer.

"Prairie chickens can be tasty," Eli told us.

Jake shot one an hour later, but his ball pretty much

exploded that bird. Wasn't much more than feathers left.

"Shame I don't have a proper bird gun," Jake said, staring at his toes.

"The trick's to do it Indian-style," Eli explained later. I was a bit bewildered, being ignorant of Indian hunting habits. Eli just grinned, waved us past the wagon, and demonstrated the finer points of prairie-chicken hunting.

Actually, there wasn't all that much to it, especially for a Tennessee boy. We were natural-born rock throwers, and that was most of it. The only halfway hard part was sneaking up on those prairie chickens. Once you got close, you walloped one senseless with your rock.

Now prairie chickens were known to wander, but mostly in summer. Once cool weather set in, they stayed put. It being November, they collected in sizable batches. Early in the morning and on toward dusk, when they were eating, you had your best shot. And if you worked some at it, you could fill up a game bag.

That first day Jake and I set off at twilight, creeping across the land, letting our shadowy selves blend into the tall grasses. We didn't exactly see or hear the birds, but I could tell something was astir up ahead. Jake led me in that direction. We had our pockets stuffed with rocks, so when we spied the prairie chickens, we were ready.

We didn't strike right away, though. There was

something about those birds, pecking at bugs, rustling around in perfect peace. Even the big ones, the males, weren't more than a foot and a half long, and the hens were even smaller. They were brownish gray mostly, but I deemed them pretty just the same. I couldn't help feeling like I was trespassing, intruding on their country. I eyed Jake, and he seemed of like mind. For a good quarter hour we lay there, watching, frozen in thought.

Finally Jake nudged me, and we went to work. It wasn't half the fun I'd expected. Even so, I went ahead and knocked down one after another. Eli told us how a fellow collected four dozen one afternoon. Jake and I settled for ten. It was enough to provide a good supper.

"It's not like shooting a deer, is it?" Jake asked when we collected our birds.

"No," I agreed. "Deer's got some kind of a chance. Still, we need the meat."

"I'd almost rather go hungry," Jake confessed. "But I wouldn't enjoy seeing Jordy and Josh get any thinner."

"No, they've gotten twig skinny."

"You're no prize hog yourself," Jake said, poking my side. "Be almost as good as Grandma's fried chicken, don't you suppose?"

"Hope so," I said, smiling. "Sure be glad when we get settled. I miss regular cooking, fresh eggs—"

"Hush!" Jake said, motioning to the dead prairie chickens. "Help collect 'em. We won't finish any faster with you jabbering away!"

The prairie chickens made for a fine supper. Baked up with spices, I believe those prairie chickens were a match for anything I'd ever eaten.

"You couldn't find their equal at the best Nashville hotel!" Pa declared.

After supper, we tended to chores. I fiddled a few tunes, after which we boys spread our blankets in a hay barn offered us by a farmer named Haskell Moore. Mr. Moore's hospitality proved to be a real stroke of luck because the night got downright disagreeable outside. A wind toppled Mr. Moore's woodpile and shredded our canvas wagon-cover. Two farms up the road even lost their roofs. I slept through every bit of it, nestled in the warm hay, with Sandy keeping my toes from freezing and one brother or another squeezed in alongside.

On Wednesday the wind persisted, and rain came down besides. A mile outside Honey Grove the wagon sank axle deep in mud, and we had to unload it in the rain. Even then it took every one of us pushing, and the Morgans straining, to coax those wheels out of their ruts. We ate prairie chickens for supper again, and that helped calm Pa, who was put out with a farmer for charging us two silver dollars for fodder.

"You'd expect oats at least for such a price!" Pa exclaimed. "Corn husks! Why, we toss such aside back home!"

"Back home?" Jordy asked. "Thought our home was Texas now."

It drew a deep frown from Pa, who stormed off to grumble in solitude.

None of us was any too cheered by Jordy's notion of home. Rain gave way to snow, and we found ourselves more often wet and discouraged than not. The mud sucked my moccasins right off my feet hourly, and the hide soles disintegrated Friday. Ma wrapped my feet in blanket strips, and Pa promised it wouldn't be much farther.

"It isn't, either," Eli assured me.

But if it hadn't been for the hospitality we found in Fannin County, I suspect I would have frozen. People there took our horses into their barn, and they gave us leave to spread our blankets beside the fireplace in their cabin. They exiled their own children to cold corners so we could enjoy a warm night.

"Don't let it trouble you," a boy named Lester said when I argued we should swap spots. "We came here ourselves a while back. I recollect winter on the trail."

I did my best to repay the kindnesses, fiddling up tunes and doing every chore I could imagine.

"I vow this, Joe," Ma remarked when we turned south from the thriving little town of Bonham and headed at last toward Collin County. "If ever a traveler comes past our new home, we'll welcome him inside no matter how empty our larder."

I don't know just when we crossed into Collin County. There was a road leading south to the Trinity crossing at Dallas, and we took it. Pa and Eli went on ahead to locate our farm, so Jake kept us rolling along at a weary if steady pace while we awaited word of our final destination.

Sandy and I scouted the surrounding country when we could. The prairie oozed with black dirt, but the few farms we saw were off the trail. It was cold, so we didn't meet other travelers or see anybody out and about.

Darkness found us still on the road, and Jake located our camp atop a knoll overlooking a shallow creek. There we erected a shelter of sorts using what was left of the wagon-cover and two old blankets. Ma cooked up some greens and baked cornbread, but we found no prairie chickens or rabbits for the stew pot.

"It shouldn't be much farther now, children," Ma said when we complained of our scant supper.

"No, ma'am," we murmured. But words don't fill your belly.

Hunger wasn't our only trouble, either. We worried about Pa and Eli. Then, just after the moon crept into the evening sky, a pair of wolves started howling.

"Go away!" Jake called to them. "Slim pickings hereabouts."

Jake then made the mistake of spinning us a tale about a wolf that liked to nibble the toes off boys. Didn't Jordy, Josh, or I sleep much the whole night. I heard a twig snap around midnight, and I jumped up, grabbed a rock, and prepared to defend my toes.

"Easy there, Jer," Eli called. "It's just me."

"Oh," I said, discarding the rock.

"What's got you so riled?" he asked, steadying my quivering shoulders.

"Been wolves about," I explained. "Hungry ones. I thought they might try to eat us."

"With Sandy about?" Eli asked, laughing.

"Sandy's asleep," I said, nodding to the slumbering collie. Where he'd guard you against a thousand road pirates, Sandy wasn't much for waking to snapping twigs.

"Come help me tend my horse," Eli suggested, and I did, even though the cold tormented my bare feet and legs. That flannel shirt didn't do all that much for the rest of me, either!

Still, I don't suspect I could have slept, what with the wolves howling in the distance.

"Don't you figure they've got a right to howl some?" Eli asked as he removed the saddle and dragged it aside. "There's easier lives than what wolves've got."

"I guess," I said. "But they bother a man's stock, you know. Hard on chickens especially."

"Sure, but I never heard one to attack a man unless it was cornered. No different than snakes."

"I'm partial to snakes," I confessed.

"Heard that," Eli said, grinning. "That's why I knew you'd understand about wolves. Truth is, out here most things'll leave you be, Jericho—if you do the same to them."

"Sure," I said, sighing. "Find our place, Eli?"

"Did," he whispered. "Left your pa there. I'll get the rest of you there tomorrow."

"What's it like?" I asked.

"You'll see for yourself soon enough."

"Tell me," I pleaded.

"No, it's best to let it surprise you," he said, squeezing my shoulders. "But I don't expect you'll be disappointed. Now let's get some rest."

I sighed and trudged along to my blankets. I didn't sleep, though. Get some rest? Eli'd been with us more than a month, and he didn't know me at all. I wasn't likely to rest much knowing our new home was so near!

Every single time I closed my eyes that night I dreamed of what the new place would be like. One moment I'd see a fine house with brick walls and a wide porch. The next time it would be a clapboard shack. We'd seen both in Texas, and every other sort of dwelling imaginable as well.

Ma roused us early that next morning.

"We're close now," she told us. "We won't even waste time on breakfast. Just pack the wagon, and let's get started!"

"Yes'm!" we cried. And before we knew it, we got the wagon packed up and the Morgans hitched. Ma allowed us a cold square of cornbread, which we nibbled as we rolled south. After traveling a mile or so, Eli led us off the main trail up a winding creek. We tensed every time a house or barn appeared up ahead, but we passed seven or eight before spying Pa. He was standing with his horse beside a small cabin on a hill overlooking the creek.

"Pa!" Josh shouted as he clambered down from the wagon and raced up the hill.

"This it?" Jordy screamed.

Ma whipped the Morgans into a trot, and the wagon cut ruts in the hillside as it hurried toward the house. She climbed down and wrapped her arms around Pa, and they danced up and down for a time.

"Looks like we're home," Jordy told me.

"Looks like it," I agreed, giving Sandy a pat on his head.

"So, youngsters, what do you think?" Pa called as he drew us close.

"Looks like a good place," Jake declared. "Lots of fields to plant, and good water nearby."

"Neighbors?" Jane Mary asked.

"Plenty," Pa answered. "And a regular school."

"Maybe we can plant some trees," I said, staring at the emptiness of the land stretching out from the creek.

"Your grandpa sent along seeds," Pa explained. "Deemed it fitting to plant trees. Offers shade. And gives a man roots."

I matched Pa's smile, and when he rested a hand on my shoulder, I leaned back against his iron-hard side.

CHAPTER TWELVE

WE DIDN'T CELEBRATE RIGHT AWAY. MA INSISTED WE should pray some, which we did. Pa recorded our arrival in the family Bible. Afterward there was unloading to get done, wood to chop, and the like. I hardly had a chance to catch my breath!

Our new home surprised me some. The house had four rooms—two on each side of a roofed porch of sorts. Twin fireplaces provided heat for the rooms. Outside, there was a coop full of chickens, a sty with three pigs, and a small barn and corral. Uncle Dan left a deed and a letter with neighbors, and Pa explained that besides the house and the land we had a wood two miles or so down the creek where he could get firewood and lumber.

Inside, we were surprised to discover a batch of rope beds with straw mattresses waiting for us. Ma had a couple of chests for her dishes and a table and chairs where we could eat.

"Civilization," she announced. "First thing tomorrow you boys will have a bath!"

"We'd best cut their hair, too," Jane Mary added. "They resemble thieves!"

"Looks like we really are home," Jake grumbled. "Sister's got her sassy tongue back!"

I laughed at that, and Jane Mary gave my arm a whack. I didn't waste a moment escaping out the door and dashing past the coop toward the barn. Sandy barked as he raced over, and I gave him a welcoming pat as he licked my fingers.

"Tomorrow we'll scare up some rabbits, eh, boy?" I whispered. He barked and wagged his tail excitedly.

I chased Sandy around the barn a time or two before Ma called me back inside. There were chores awaiting my attention. In fact, I was pretty well occupied the rest of the day and didn't get back outside until after supper.

The air was crisp and cool, and darkness was settling in. I shook off the wind's bite and concentrated on the stars sparkling overhead. You couldn't make out all of them yet, but the evening star was there, and others were popping up each minute.

"Texas has wide skies, doesn't it?" Pa called to me from the porch.

"Yes, sir," I agreed, trotting over and sitting with him on the steps.

"Air's got a sweet taste to it, too. Good black earth," he observed as he dug his fingers into the ground and scooped up a handful of mud. "We'll grow some fine things here."

"Lots of corn," I said, nodding my head. "Peaches after a time."

"Sure, we'll manage those. Mostly we'll grow Wetherbys, though. Good men to build this new state of ours. How's that notion settle with you, Jericho?"

"Figure even I'll grow?" I asked, staring at a bright star directly overhead.

"All things grow," he assured me. "Even a peach tree starts out as a seed. I figure you past sapling stage already, son, and sure to stretch yourself directly. Already got the heart to make a good one. Proved that on the journey."

"I did?"

"Not much fearful of bridges anymore, I've noticed. Even shoeless, you kept on the trail. Fair at fiddling even. A journey tests the makings of a man, you know. Recall those folks who turned back?"

"The ones that left Texas?" I asked.

"I had a plow once that cut deep furrows through loose dirt, but come across rough ground, it was less than no use. Those folks that turned away from Texas broke themselves against the rocks, so to speak. Didn't have enough inside to stomach hardship and disappointment."

134

"Does anyone?" I asked.

"I think so, Jericho," Pa said, turning my head so that he could study my eyes. "And I number you among 'em. The important thing's whether you number yourself one or not."

"I'm only twelve, Pa. I'm not sure."

"Yes, you are," he said, squeezing my neck. "I knew that when you saved your dog back in Tennessee. And so did you, I suspect."

"Guess you're right," I said, chewing the words and finding them to my liking. "But you won't expect me to be altogether grown up just yet?"

"No, I figure you for a prank now and again," he said, grinning.

I wrapped an arm around his thick side, and we sat together silently on the porch another few minutes.

"Morning comes early for farm boys, you know," he whispered as he got to his feet. "Even in Texas."

"Especially in Texas," Ma called from the door. "Jericho, best you ready your bed. Your brothers are waiting on you."

"Yes, ma'am," I said, rising. And though I generally disliked such chores, I didn't half mind helping Jordy spread blankets across the straw mattress we were to share. I knew that night we'd enjoy the warmth of a fire, the comfort of our own bed, and the wonderful sense of belonging that came with a journey's end— and a new home.